Stiletto
Silver

A GREAT ~~~
EROTIC NOVELS FEATURING
FEMALE DOMINANTS

If you like one you will probably like the rest

A NEW TITLE EVERY MONTH

Stiletto Readers Service
c/o Silver Moon Books Ltd
109A Roundhay Road
Leeds, LS8 5AJ

http://www.electronicbookshops.com

Silver Moon Books of Leeds and New York are in no way connected with Silver Moon Books of London

If you like one of our books you will probably like them all!

Stiletto Reader Services
c/o Silver Moon Books Ltd
109A Roundhay Road
Leeds, LS8 5AJ

http://www.electronicbookshops.com

New authors welcome
Please send submissions to
STILETTO
Silver Moon Books Ltd.
PO Box 5663
Nottingham
NG3 6PJ

Stocks and Bonds first published 2000, copyright John Angus

The right of John Angus to be identified as the author of this book has been asserted in accordance with Section 77 and 78 of the Copyrights and Patents Act 1988

STOCKS and BONDS
by
John Angus

This is fiction - In real life always practise safe sex!

CHAPTER ONE

The last thing Peter Cross wanted to see on a Monday morning was "error 23" flickering on his computer screen. He'd spent half the weekend working on the Talisan project and all of it was on the little diskette which his miserable excuse for a computer was obstinately refusing to read.

He ordered it to try again and got the same result. Furiously, he banged his fingers down on the enter key and ordered it to read the thing again and again, getting angrier at each successive failure.

He yanked the disk out and left his cubicle, walking down to see Dennis Baxter.

"Dennis? Would you try this in your machine, please?" he asked, leaning into his messy little walled-off cubicle.

Dennis looked up from his keyboard and grinned, then took the disk and slipped it into his slot.

"Hello, there."

They both turned as Michael Rose, computer engineering supervisor, appeared at the entrance to Baxter's cubicle along with an attractive blonde neither of them knew.

She was quite tall, with large shoulders and an impressive figure. She wore a tight, black business suit with a very short skirt, and Peter caught Dennis discreetly eyeing her long legs as the woman looked over his messy cubicle.

"Peter Cross and Dennis Baxter, this is Kathleen Hunter, my replacement, your new supreme ruler and general all around deity."

"How do you do?" Kathleen said, her voice deep, her pronunciation flawlessly upper class. She stood proud and erect, surveying the two men with a critical and experienced gaze.

"Peter and Dennis work on the Talisan project," Michael said.

"I shall look forward to meeting with both of you personally," Kathleen said, her piercing eyes moving from one to the other then back again.

Peter felt them lock onto him, and felt a strange sense of helplessness, as though Kathleen was examining his very soul. He felt an instinctive urge to back away for the woman exuded such power and strength. Somehow, instinctively, he knew the woman was not going to be like the gentle, good-natured Rose and that she would not be someone to cross or to argue with.

Rose led her on and Dennis shook his head. "Cor, what a looker. What legs! And did you see those tits of hers?"

"I don't think you better let her hear you talking about her like that, Dennis," Peter said thoughtfully.

"You got that right, son. That's one cold fish there. You hear her accent? Right out of bloody Oxford is my guess."

"Too old."

"She's not that old. Maybe thirty or so. Not a lot older. Anyway, I didn't mean she just bloody graduated I meant..."

"I know."

"And what's with the hair?" he turned and grinned at Peter slyly. "You know, you just don't often see grown women with hair that short. Not in this business."

"Maybe she finds it easier to wash," Peter said, not sure why he was trying to defend the woman.

"More likely she's a ruddy dyke."

"That's not the kind of word you need to be caught using either," Peter said dryly.

"So turn me in to the PC thought police."

He grinned and turned back to his computer, hitting a few keys.

"Just because she's gay - that is, if she is gay, is no reason for you to think she's some kind of...well, some kind of sexual raver or something."

"Just you wait," Dennis muttered.

He turned and handed Peter another disk with his program on it.

"Oh, you could read it? Lovely. I wonder why mine wouldn't."

"Happens sometimes," he said with a shrug. "Nobody seems to know why. Just be glad everything's not wrecked."

"I am. Thanks very much."

He went back to his cubicle to call up the program.

He kept thinking about Kathleen Hunter though. There was something decidedly odd about the woman. It wasn't her sexual orientation either. Peter agreed with Dennis that there was a good chance the woman was a lesbian, but that didn't bother him. No. It was something else again.

Dennis had described her as cold. But that wasn't quite it. Peter could easily believe the woman was a strict disciplinarian. The way those eyes had pierced him, had pinned him down like a bird examining a worm had been startling. He'd never felt so insignificant, like a serf before a queen.

What, he wondered, would such a woman be like in bed?

Absurd to think about, of course. The woman probably was a lesbian. And yet that only served to excite him more. The thought of Kathleen with another woman, another tall, beautiful woman, their slim, nude bodies sliding together, soft flesh caressing soft flesh, breasts crushing breasts...

He was fully erect now, his cock hard along the leg of this thigh, pressing up against the thin fabric of his trousers. His fingers sat on his keyboard, but his mind was filled with images of the stern, cool Kathleen Hunter.

What if she wasn't a lesbian. God, he thought. She would be hard to impress. She'd never settle for the likes of him anyway. Oh, he knew he was a handsome man, boyishly good looking, with a charming smile. He spent a considerable effort working out to keep trim and fit. But a woman like Kathleen Hunter could draw in whatever rich, handsome men she wanted. She'd have no need of a lowly systems programmer like him.

He hadn't a lot of experience with women, but he had a large, thick cock, and thought he knew fairly well how to use it. But Kathleen Hunter had a look in her eyes like she'd seen it all and then some more. Displeasing her, he felt certain, would not be met with calm acceptance - more animal-like venom and revenge.

He cursed and tried to shake his mind free of the foolish daydream. He had work to do, and God alone knew what would happen if someone called him away and he was forced to stand up with his cock pressing out against his trousers like it was.

He tried to continue work on the project and forget about Kathleen Hunter, and eventually succeeded. He had lunch with Stephen Reilly and Michael Simms though, and they were both eager to know what he thought of the impressive Kathleen Hunter.

No sooner had he returned than he got a phone call from the woman himself, asking him - though the tone left little doubt that asking was a polite fiction - to come to her office and see her.

He felt a little nervous as he rose and ran his hands through his short brown hair. He looked at himself in his small mirror, swallowed, and then walked down the aisle between the cubicles to Kathleen's glass-windowed office.

Peter saw that the shades were all closed. Michael had always kept the windows clear. He knocked on the door and Kathleen's imperious voice called out for him to enter.

The office had undergone a drastic change since the morning. No longer was it filled with soft, old-fashioned wooden furniture. Now everything was gleaming chrome, leather and glass. Kathleen sat behind a large glass and steel desk, talking on the phone as she typed at her computer terminal. She pointed at one of the small leather and steel chairs before her desk without pausing, and Peter sat carefully.

"I don't care what he wants," Kathleen said firmly. She paused for a moment. "No. I said no! Did you not hear me? I do not care what he wants. You'll do it this way now. If you aren't capable of it we'll find another supplier."

She hung up and turned to Peter, lips pursed as she examined him silently. Then she pulled over a folder and opened it. "Peter Cross," she stated.

"Yes," Peter said, barely restraining himself from saying 'ma'am'.

"You've been with us four years. Got a number of good reports."

Peter nodded and tried to smile. Kathleen's cool eyes froze the attempt in a chilling yet not threatening glare.

"Not married. No children. Good. You won't be out partying all the time and no brats to stay home and care for."

She stood up and began to pace, her long lean legs and wriggling backside moving within the confines of her tight skirt to accentuate her slim shape beneath.

"As you are no doubt aware, computer engineering is by far the largest and most important part of this company. The other sections are just there to provide for us, to market our products, take care of bookkeeping, perform clerical duties and so on."

She looked at Peter for confirmation of his attention and understanding. He nodded his response.

"We only have two hundred and forty employees, so having another level of management above the supervisor of computer engineering is superfluous. The owners have agreed then that in addition to being head of computer engineering I'm also to be the titular president of the company, responsible only to the board."

Peter nodded again, uncertain as to why he was being

treated to this little lecture.

"I aim to change the perception of this company. It's going to be one of youth and vitality, of sexual excitement and glitter, futuristic and on the cutting edge. I want people to speak of us with awe. I want people lining up to come and work for us, the youngest people, the brightest and most brilliant and most daring."

She whirled suddenly and bent, causing Peter to pull his head back in alarm at the suddenness of her movement.

"Do you think you fit in with that image?"

"Well I..."

"Because not everyone will. I've already let a number of people go."

"Y-You have?" Peter stammered.

"Perception is everything in this business. And ours is in for a drastic change. You can be part of that or not as the case may be."

He had just moved into a new flat in South Lambeth, one whose payments he could just barely afford on his present salary. He felt a knot of tension grip him as he nodded hesitantly.

Kathleen straightened and looked at him doubtfully. "Comb your hair."

"Excuse me?" Peter stared at her in confusion.

"Your hair. You look like a bloody schoolmaster like that."

Peter's hair was neatly cut, parted on one side, just as it had been when he was a boy. He wasn't at all sure what the woman was on about but felt too intimidated to say so.

"Well I - that is ..."

Kathleen's hands slipped suddenly into his hair, combing it straight back from his forehead. She muttered something, dipped her fingers into a glass of water on her desk, and then shoved them through his hair again, raking it back still further.

"Yes, better," she said, as he looked at her in astonishment.

"Much more mod. But those clothes!"

She shook her head and made a face.

"I do hope you've got something more hip, something more modern and sexy. We have to up-beat our image."

"I...well...I mean. I've always dressed in a businesslike fashion."

"Our business is selling our software. Since our products aren't much different from everyone else's software we need to sell ourselves, sell the company. You think this is the most comfortable outfit I could have chosen to wear to work today?" she demanded, indicating her own tight, short skirt and blouse. She posed for his benefit, allowing him a long and leisurely leer at her shape.

"From now on you will dress stylishly; tight pants, good, tailored jackets, silk ties. I want a modern look, you understand? I don't want anything that makes you look like your daddy did. All the men will be dressing the same way, in nice snappy trousers and shirts, silks and colours. I'm not having any scruffy jeans and beards either. Anyone who doesn't want to shape up can ship himself or herself off."

"You honestly expect men like Dennis Baxter to make like some flashy..."

"Baxter is gone."

Peter stared at her in shock, his mouth open and eyes wide in disbelief.

"Gave him his walking papers during lunch."

"But - but..."

"I can hand you the same if you want."

Peter bit his lip.

"So. I can count on you?" she demanded in a tone that simply challenged a refusal.

Peter nodded helplessly.

"Good. Don't let me see you in here in some old banker's outfit tomorrow or else I'll put you across my lap and spank that pretty bottom of yours."

She cocked her head slightly to one side and let her lips curl upwards, and Peter felt his face flush as butterflies joined the knot in his stomach.

"Look, Peter," she said, sliding her arm over Peter's shoulder, "I'm not trying to be a brute. Honestly. But this company is bleeding money and someone's got to take drastic action."

Peter was uncomfortably aware of Kathleen's heavy breast pushing against his shoulder as the blonde walked him to the door. Uncomfortable because his groin was stirring, and he felt a deathly terror that he would spring erect right in front of the woman.

"I'm strict and demanding but I am fair. If I must discipline you," she said, turning and then cocking her finger under Peter's chin to pull his face up, "you'll know why and get a chance to say your piece."

She smiled, and then eased her fingers back, sliding them ever so lightly along Peter's cheek, through his hair, then back as she opened the door.

"Come and see me any time," she said softly in parting.

Peter walked back to his cubicle in a daze, barely noting the empty one where Dennis had worked.

Everything the woman said made sense. The company was in trouble, with no name to speak of and nothing much to differentiate it from its more famous competitors. Young, sleek, and sexy might well change that.

And she'd even been sort of, well, nice there at the end. Peter wondered if she really was a lesbian, and considered that business where she'd touched his chin and hair. Did Kathleen fancy him?

He felt a wave of shocked excitement at the thought. His cock sprang instantly erect once again and he swallowed nervously as he sat down. Kathleen Hunter was an incredibly impressive woman! She was hardly a woman at all. She was so much above women it would be like... like having sex with an entirely different gender!

So smart and beautiful and strong! Naked, she would be magnificent! And Peter indulged himself by imagining them arm in arm, their lips sliding together, his cock driving upwards into her tightness.

Yet the idea was absurd, and he pushed it far from his mind as he turned to the computer and got back to work.

It kept intruding, though. Odd flashes and images of Kathleen and he embracing, lips touching, naked, kept appearing out of nowhere, disturbing and distracting him.

***

The next two weeks were frantic at work, with a large turnover of employees, new projects instituted and old ones dumped. Much of it was exasperating to Peter, yet he found himself watching Kathleen, feeling his admiration for the woman growing by the day.

Kathleen Hunter was incredibly energetic, filled with ideas, and a strict enough taskmistress to see them carried out. She changed everything from the sign out front of the building to the colour of the diskettes they shipped their software on. She also came up with a number of brilliant innovations that had the staff shaking their heads.

She came out among the staff much more often than Rose had. When her heavy, padded leather door wasn't closed she was often out peering over the shoulders of this or that employee, whispering encouraging words into their ears.

So Peter told himself there was nothing special about the tall blonde coming into his cubicle, slipping a hand over his shoulder and looking at his screen as she talked to him in a low, throaty voice.

But he was exquisitely aware of how close she was each time, of her perfume in his nose and her soft voice next to his ear. And the strange visions he kept getting became lewd, erotic fantasies, which disturbed and aroused him.

The idea of anything between them was preposterous! He wasn't in Kathleen's class. It would be like a mouse having a relationship with a cat.

And surely nothing should really be made of the quick pecks on the cheek Kathleen sometimes gave him before she left, especially when she was happy with something Peter had done.

Peter squirmed nonetheless, becoming flustered and tongue tied around his boss to the point he could only sit silently and try not to say anything stupid whenever the woman came into his little cubicle.

When he was called into the office on Friday he was filled with anxiety, not of what Kathleen would do, but of what he himself might say that might be stupid and give away the bizarre fascination he was feeling towards his boss.

"Close the door," Kathleen ordered calmly but positively.

Peter obeyed quickly, and then stood before her desk feeling like a guilty schoolboy.

"Your delivery on the McMann project was to be made this morning."

"I know," Peter said apologetically. "I had problems..."

Kathleen held up her hand to halt his excuses.

"I read your email. I don't accept the reasons. This is not a complex task and you've done it before. You gave me a time and date it would be ready. Both were reasonable. Both were achievable. You didn't keep your promise."

Peter bit his lip worriedly. Kathleen was right, of course. His excuses were just that. He simply hadn't been his old self these past two weeks, and hadn't been working like his old self. He was distracted and slow and he now cursed himself for even attempting to put a series of half-baked excuses over on her.

"I'm sorry," he said, feeling both embarrassed and miserable for letting Kathleen down.

"That doesn't cut it. I needed that program so I could do the interface in time to present it Monday. Now I don't have it. How are you going to make that up to me?"

Peter shrugged helplessly, uneasy, his face red.

"No idea?" she prompted icily.

"I..."

"Could work all weekend."

Peter opened his mouth, and then closed it abruptly.

"Could stay here this evening late, come in tomorrow early and stay all day and well into the evening," she added in a rapid flow that momentarily confused him.

Peter nodded helplessly.

"And what guarantee do I have you'll keep your project dates even then?"

"I will! I promise! There really isn't much left to do."

"You'll have the program written before you go home Saturday and debugged by Sunday noon?"

Peter nodded his head quickly.

"That will mean I shall have to come in Sunday to work on the interface."

"I'm sorry," Peter said miserably.

"Apologies don't do a thing for me, my dear."

Kathleen rose and came around the desk. She reached out and took Peter's chin, holding it firmly and looking into his eyes.

Peter trembled slightly, not meeting her eyes, averting his gaze so as not to feel even guiltier.

"Look at me," Kathleen demanded.

Peter obeyed, and Kathleen studied him intently.

"What's been in your mind these past weeks, hmm? What's got you so befuddled?"

"N-nothing," Peter breathed.

"Problem with a girl?" she probed knowingly.

Peter numbly shook his head, mouth dry.

Kathleen's hand slid up his cheek, then combed slowly through his hair.

"You sure?" she probed further in a soft and coaxing voice.

Peter nodded breathlessly, feeling his heart pounding.

"All right. Go back to your desk then, love. I suppose missing the weekend will be enough punishment for you."

She bent to peck him on the cheek and Peter jerked his head back suddenly. Their lips met for a moment before Kathleen pulled back, eyes widening slightly, and then narrowing. Peter's face warmed and he looked away desperately.

"Go on then," Kathleen said, after looking at him a long moment.

She eased back, then gave Peter a sharp slap on the behind as he started for the door. Peter gasped and jerked forward a step or two, but didn't look back as he fled the office.

He went back to work, but if anything he was more distracted. By the time everyone started leaving he had accomplished virtually nothing. By seven he was the only one left in his section, though the light was still on in Kathleen's office.

He looked up at the little stuffed panda, which beamed down from atop his monitor and sighed miserably. Would this be...could this be the result of his lucky charm?

He prayed Kathleen wouldn't stop by before leaving, stop by and see how little he had done. He was already dreadfully unhappy and embarrassed about his poor performance and didn't want to do anything else to lower Kathleen's opinion of him.

But, of course, Kathleen did come out of her office and

did wander down the aisle to Peter's cubicle. Peter was rigid with tension as the woman walked in and bent over behind him.

"Well?"

"I-it's coming along," he gulped.

"What line number?"

Peter didn't answer and Kathleen reached over and typed in a query, then made an angry sound.

"This is all you've done?"

"I-I'm sorry," Peter said in a small voice.

"You certainly are!" she stood up, glaring. "Come to my office."

Peter followed her back to her office, expecting to be fired but, oddly, more upset that he'd made Kathleen think he was such a lazy incompetent fool.

Kathleen shoved him into the room and closed the door behind her, then pulled him over to the sofa and sat down with him, her bare leg almost touching his.

"Must you always turn your head away?" Kathleen demanded in exasperation, the irritation that she felt sounding all too clearly in her tone.

As she'd done before she slipped her fingers beneath Peter's chin and turned his head around to face her. Peter's eyes fluttered like small birds as Kathleen stared at him. His chest felt so tight he could hardly breath, and butterflies fluttered around his stomach in a very unpleasant manner.

"Confession is good for the soul," she soothed huskily.

"I - don't know what..."

"What's in your pretty little head, hmm? Is it me?"

Pretty? She thought he was pretty? Peter felt only a mild tinge of indignation at the word as his heart leapt with pleasure.

"You? No!" he said a little too quickly in deflection.

"No? Not even a little? Nothing I've done?"

Peter shook his head; he flushed under her scrutinising gaze.

"You're not feeling uneasy working for a woman?"

"No," Peter gulped.

"Sure?"

Peter tried to nod his head but Kathleen's fingers kept his chin up.

"Have you been thinking naughty thoughts about me?"

Peter began to tremble slightly.

"I realise that you're married but you're acting awfully odd around me."

"I - don't know what you mean," Peter breathed.

"No?"

Kathleen turned her head slightly, then her hand slipped from his chin, sliding along the side of his cheek, stroking it delicately as she leaned in. Peter looked away; his heart threatening to burst as he felt Kathleen's lips gently brush the nape of his neck.

"No?" Kathleen whispered.

Her lips traced a hot trail upwards along his neck, then over his cheek. Then she kissed him softly on the lips. She eased back a moment, smiled, then kissed him again, her arms sliding around him as she let her weight bear him back against the back of the sofa.

Her hand slipped lightly through Peter's hair, stroking it slowly as she kissed him softly, her lips pressing in, then back, sliding along Peter's, and then trailing along the nape of his neck.

Peter did nothing but gulp in air, his body overheating, sweat oozing from every pore as he felt his body tremble with excitement. He felt his cock stiff and erect, thrusting up against his tight trousers as Kathleen's hand slid down, lightly slipping past without touching it, stroking his thigh as she purred like a cat.

Kathleen's lips found his again, and this time he hesitantly kissed back, a thrilled sexual heat rolling up and down his body, making his insides burn.

He shuddered as Kathleen's hand stroked his chest, nimbly undoing the top two buttons of his shirt to slip inside and caress his bare skin. Kathleen pushed his head back harder, her lips pushing in firmly now and her tongue dipping into Peter's mouth.

Abruptly, she turned, twisted, and straddled him, then, as he gaped up breathlessly, she ripped his shirt open, sending the rest of the buttons flying across the room. She gripped his hair, yanking his head back, causing him to cry out in pain. Then her lips were in against his exposed throat, chewing and suckling as she growled lightly.

He felt her weight on his groin, her taut buttocks grinding against his stiff erection, and moaned helplessly, awash in sexual need and desire, his mind swimming against a torrent of helpless lust.

Peter felt almost dazed with shock and excitement. It seemed impossible that this was happening, that he, dull, mousy Peter Cross was engaging in anything so shocking and exciting as a sexual interlude with his gorgeous employer in her own office.

"Oh! I... Oh!"

Kathleen had slid slightly down his body, enough to gnaw at his nipples, chewing and licking at them with a long, wet, warm tongue. Peter was flabbergasted. He had never seen a woman like this, never imagined to experience one. His own sexual escapades in the past were mild and utterly common, consisting almost entirely of missionary position sex with young women who appeared contented and pleased, but hardly anything like this.

Kathleen chewed her way back up to his throat even as

her hands dived for his belt, undoing it and ripping it free. Then, before he could react, she had slipped the belt around his shoulders, down just above his elbows, and then yanked it tight.

He stared stupidly as his arms were pinned to his sides, watching as a cool smile slid across her face.

"Naughty boy," she said. "You'll have to be punished, you realise that don't you?"

He heard a soft, animal groan and realised it was him.

Kathleen leaned back, undoing his trousers, then slipped off him, yanking them down his hips along with his shorts, pulling his legs up and out before him by sheer strength as she ripped the trousers and shorts down and off, sending his shoes flying.

She smirked at the sight of him and his face reddened. He sat on her sofa naked but for his socks, his cock stiff, standing up like a flagpole.

She rose, appearing to tower above him.

"Come here," she ordered coldly.

Face burning, he started to rise, but she pointed down.

"On your knees, dog."

Another thrill tore through him, and he groaned again as he slid to his knees, making no effort to free his pinned arms. He shuffled across, mind floating on a sexual high the likes of which he had never before felt.

"Lean across the stool there," she ordered.

Peter saw the low, padded footstool and shuffled there, bending over, groaning as she squatted low behind him and let her hand caress his bottom.

"You have a lovely ass, do you know that, sweetie?" she said calmly.

Then her hand smacked against his flesh hard enough to make him cry out and he jerked against the stool.

She laughed, and then gripped his cock. He felt a wave of pleasure and heat and his hips ground helplessly downwards. Her other hand slapped his backside again.

"Be still," she ordered curtly.

This was all madness, Peter thought, dazed at the events of the last few minutes, shocked and hardly daring to credit that this was not a bizarre dream.

Kathleen showed him a small piece of bent tubing, and he wondered, for a moment, what it could possibly mean. Then his legs were being pushed apart, and her hand pushed the U-shaped piece of metal against the side of the stool. He felt it slide in on either side of his cock as it hung just above the edge of the stool. Then, somehow, it was forced into the side of the stool, forced in hard so that it pinned his cock against the soft wood just below his testicles.

He groaned as the metal pushed against his stiff, hard erection, and instinctively jerked back, only to find himself held in place, his testicles throbbing as they pulled against the metal.

Her hand pushed against the back of his head, bending him over again, and another hard slap to the buttocks sent a sharp pain through his body.

"Are you sorry for disappointing me, Peter?" she demanded.

"Y-Yes!" he gasped.

Her hand cracked against his bottom again.

"Yes mistress."

His heart gave a lurch.

"Yes mistress," he breathed, stunned.

Her hand cracked against his bottom again and his hips jerked, first downwards, as if trying to jam more of his cock through the tight ring of metal holding him in place, then back, as if to pull himself free.

He felt a sense of humiliation at his position, at what he

had allowed the woman to do to him. She was still fully clothed, perfectly coiffured, her makeup in place. And yet here he was naked and bent over, his stiff cock pinned against the side of a stool, his rump raised towards her.

She stood up and he raised his head to follow her movements, eyes staring hungrily at the lithe body hidden beneath her short skirt and tight blouse. She opened a cupboard and drew out a small thin paddle, then turned to him.

He realised her intention, and his face burned as shame mixed with arousal.

"You will be punished for failing to do as you were told," she said sternly.

His mouth opened and closed to protest, but no words emerged, even as she moved behind him. How could he protest when he had already allowed her to...

Crack!

"Owww!"

His backside stung fiercely, and he yanked against the metal pinning him in place, groaning as he felt his balls squeezed and crushed. He hastily threw his hips forward again even as the paddle struck his bottom once again.

He cried out again, but quickly suppressed it. It was only a paddle, after all, and he had had worse when he was a boy. He just didn't remember the pain being quite so sharp.

The paddle came down again, and he felt more shame, yet still more excitement. He had never been involved in anything, which could properly be described as kinky or perverted, but he had had fantasies, fantasies he had never dared try to bring to fruition, fantasies he barely admitted to himself.

Another blow, and more pain, and then more again.

"Silly little boy," Kathleen purred. "Did you think you could make excuses to me for your pathetically inept work?"

"N-No," he panted.

Abruptly he felt a hard pressure against his cock as her foot slipped between his thighs. The sole of her shoe was crushing his stiffened prick against the stool, and he groaned in a strange mixture of pain and pleasure.

"Mistress," she corrected.

"Mistress!" he cried.

"You have much potential, little dog," she said.

Peter felt a burst of elation, and then shuddered as her sole moved from side to side, grinding against his cock in a delicious, unbearable way, the head of his organ feeling ready to explode even without being touched.

She drew her foot back.

"Raise your bottom more," she commanded, "and spread your legs for me."

Face burning, he obeyed, breathless with a sweltering sexual heat. He felt her foot against his bottom, directly between his buttocks.

"Would you like to be my little pet?" she asked.

"I-I...y-yes, mistress," he stuttered dazedly.

"You're sure," she purred, stretching out the word.

"I..."

He felt the heel of her shoe pressing lightly against his rectum, felt it dipping in with more and more pressure, pushing slowly down into his body. He trembled and groaned, helplessly bucking against the stool, his testicles yanking against the metal pin again and again.

"You need someone to look after you, don't you, little one?"

Her heel was fully inside him. It was quite thin, but five inches in length, and she slid it slowly in and out, her foot remaining on his backside as she spoke.

"Yes, perhaps after we instil a little discipline in you we'll see if you aren't more use to us."

Peter moaned and trembled, trying to control himself. But

it was too much. He exploded, crying out in maddened pleasure as he rutted against the pin holding him in place, spurting out his seed onto the expensive carpet below as pain and pleasure twisted within his body.

He heard her throaty chuckle as he collapsed, gasping for breath, across the stool, then the paddle cracked against his buttocks again.

"Naughty boy. Look at the mess you've made on my carpet."

His face flamed and he wondered, with the sudden release of sexual tension and lust, how he had managed to allow himself to be put into such a situation. The paddle cracked down again, and his body jerked.

"Please!" he gasped.

Again the paddle lashed down.

"Mistress," she said sternly.

"I...but... I-I..."

Again the paddle smacked against his backside, and he gasped in pain.

"Mistress! Please, mistress I..."

Another blow followed, and another then he groaned, struggling to free his arms, pulling against the ring pinning him to the stool.

"Are you going to do a better job for me in future?" she demanded.

"Yes! I-I... yes, mistress!" he exclaimed.

She chuckled again and he closed his eyes in shame.

"We'll see, little boy."

She unfastened the ring binding him to the stool, and then freed his arms. A moment later she thrust a handful of tissues into his hand.

"Clean up your mess," she ordered.

Mortified, he bent and used the tissues to clean up the effects of his orgasm, then turned, half-heartedly trying to cover his groin with his hand.

"Now go back to your desk and get to work."

"But...now?" He blinked his eyes in confusion.

"Now," she ordered.

He stood up awkwardly, looking for his clothing, but saw no sign of it.

"You don't need clothes," she said with a smirk. "The building is empty.

"You can't be serious," he exclaimed.

She smiled again, and then slapped his face lightly. He stumbled back a step in shock.

"Don't question my orders," she said.

She went to the door and opened it, then pointed. "Go! And take that with you."

She wrinkled her nose in disgust at the tissues clutched in his hand.

Such was her manner that he could hardly contemplate disobedience, and before he realised it he was outside in the larger office with the door closed behind him.

And he was naked, but for his socks, the lights bright overhead. He hurried nervously to his cubicle, feeling some small measure of protection once within its confines.

How, he wondered, had he had been drawn into such a situation?

CHAPTER TWO

Peter sat down gingerly in his chair, feeling decidedly odd, wary of every sound in case it should be someone coming. When did the cleaners arrive, he wondered? What about security? What would happen if he were found nude at his desk? He could hardly dare to think about the humiliation.

He gazed at his computer, but simply could not think about working. His mind was reeling, and his heart was still beating madly. What a bizarre affair that had been!

Affair? He could hardly call it that, now could he? Kathleen hadn't even disrobed. He hadn't even really touched her. What kind of a woman was she? Why hadn't she at least, well, wanted them to do something together? Perhaps he disgusted her? He felt a wave of anxiety at the thought. Yet she had called him pretty, had obviously wanted him for... well, for what she had done. Surely she wanted more from him than that.

Next time, as soon as possible, he would do much more. He would strip her naked and feast his eyes on her magnificent body. He would make her cry out in pleasure. He would...

"Working hard?" her voice called from across the room.

"Y-yes," he gasped, fingers leaping to the keyboard.

Moments later she appeared at the entrance to his cubicle.

He turned his chair, gasping anxiously, and she glowered at him.

"Well?"

"Uhmmm, yes?"

She moved forward, and her right foot rose, coming down on the edge of his chair between his thighs, nudging his limp penis.

"If I look at that screen will I see any progress?"

His face flushed. "No, er, mistress," he whispered.

Her foot ground forward, and he winced as it mashed lightly against his penis. Yet he felt himself stirring, felt himself hardening as excitement began to thrum through his veins again. The ache was sharp, yet his chest was growing tight with sexual electricity, his breathing short and ragged.

"Flighty little thing like you probably can't concentrate now for all the excitement he's had," she said with amused contempt. "Isn't that true, Peter?"

He swallowed repeatedly, not daring to reach down to grasp

her ankle as her foot ground against him with still more pressure. He was hard now, and the burning pain of her foot grinding his cock down into the fabric of the chair had his fingernails digging into the palms of his hands.

"I...I'm trying," he gulped.

"Not hard enough. You're too busy thinking of other things, aren't you? Thinking about me naked, thinking about sucking on my nipples and sliding that big cock of yours up into my pussy. That's what you want, isn't it, Peter?"

"Yes...m-mistress," he gasped.

She pulled her foot back and he groaned in relief.

"Stand up."

He stood at once, his cock springing out red and purple before him, pointing straight at her. It embarrassed him, this so-visible sign of his helpless arousal yet it aroused him as well, for she was looking at it and could not possibly avoid seeing it, she would have to know how aroused he was - for her. He did not have to pretend with her, did not have to beat about the bush, did not have to make small, flattering remarks in hopes of being noticed. He was thrillingly erect and naked, and his want for her was blatant.

She reached down for it, folding her fingers around its girth and squeezing, then tugging him forward, using it as a lever to pull him aside. He moaned softly at the pressure of her fist around him, shuffling eagerly where she pulled. She sat in his chair, and then pulled him forward again, up to the side of the chair. His feet stumbled against the legs as she pulled harder, and he half fell across her lap.

"That's it, Peter, all the way," she said calmly.

She grasped his hair and forced him down further as he cried out in pain. His head went across the chair and hung upside down on the other side, his toes awkwardly seeking support on the floor as her hands caressed his upturned bottom.

"Naughty boy," she said.

And then she began to spank him, spank him as though he were a little boy, spank him in this most awkward and humiliating position. And he could not help but cry out as her hand smacked against his soft skin. Nor could he stop the throbbing in his penis as his excitement rose in tandem with his pain and humiliation.

What if someone saw him like this? What if a cleaner or security guard, responding to the noise, came in and found him being spanked naked across this woman's lap?

And then her hand stopped spanking long enough to slip between his trembling thighs, grasp his cock and squeeze, and he shuddered and groaned aloud.

"So easy, you men," she said in contempt. "Such prisoners to your lust."

She continued to spank him then, and his backside grew hotter and more painful as he winced and struggled to remain silent, struggled to show no response, to cling to some marginal thought of pride in his manhood. Yet the burning was beginning to become quite painful, his entire bottom hot and throbbing, the sharpness of the pain each time her hand cracked down deeper still. Peter was not used to pain, nor even discomfort. His life was one of ease and contentment, not struggle and strength.

"P-please," he heard himself whine.

She grasped his hair again; yanking his head up, then thrust him off so that he half fell onto his backside on the floor.

"Your problem, young man, is you've got too much energy," she said, looking down at him. "You need to work off that energy.

He stared at her dumbly, gulping in air, his bottom aching and sore against the rough material of the carpeting beneath.

She stood up and motioned that he should do the same.

"Get rid of those socks," she said in irritation.

He hurried to obey, then gasped as she took his cock in her hand again and moved out of the cubicle. He followed, panting and groaning somewhat as she pulled him along beside her. She walked quickly to the main door leading out into the rotunda, and then opened it.

"Not out there!"

She ignored his protest, pulling him out into the hall.

The open offices, which made up the building, formed a semi-circle around a three story high rotunda at the main entrance. Wide balconies circled the rotunda, with concrete banisters and tiled flooring. Below, in the lobby, the security desk faced the front entrance and at it sat the security guard, apparently reading a book.

He did not look up as they walked along on the third floor balcony, Peter's feet shuffling awkwardly on the cold tile, Kathleen's heels clipping lightly as she strode forward. Peter's head swivelled from side to side, his heart pounding as he waited in terror for someone to come out of one of the side offices and see him there naked. Yet his cock was harder, stiffer than ever. To be naked like this out in the open, out in the middle of the building, where anyone could see, was shockingly outrageous.

It reminded him of his youth, when he had stripped naked near his family's country home, and become instantly aroused merely by being nude out of doors. He had walked slowly and ever so warily through the woods, his feet feeling the cold earth beneath as his erection bounced before him.

And here he was in the middle of the building! Utterly naked!

Kathleen pushed into the gymnasium, a small exercise area set aside for the staff. It was carpeted in blue, and had a number of modern exercise machines to help the staff keep in shape. She pushed him against one and let go of his cock, which continued to throb and pulse.

"Start with this one. You have a nice body, Peter, but it could be better. I want to see you developing your shoulders and pectoral muscles more."

"Shouldn't I... get dressed?" he asked weakly.

"I like to see you as you are," she said with a smug smile, propping herself against another machine and flicking her eyes up and down his body.

Flushing, he obeyed, and began to work the machine, pumping his arms up and down, pulling on the padded levers as she watched. His cock remained rigid below him as he worked, the very air seeming to caress it with taunting fingers as he moved and it bobbled and jerked between his legs.

Kathleen watched for a time, then slid forward and came across to him. Her hands slid slowly over his arms and chest as he worked, fingers caressing his skin.

"Very nice start," she said, feeling the play of muscles below his skin. "But you'll need to improve. I want to see better definition on your pecs and stomach."

Her hand slid down between his legs and gave his cock a squeeze, then pulled. He gasped, letting her pull him away from the machine and across the room to where a chin-up bar hung. She let go and nodded towards it, watching as he reached up, grasped the bar and slowly pulled himself up off his feet.

He gasped and almost fell as her hand slipped down between his buttocks and squeezed him, and he heard a chuckle from her.

"You don't mind my touching you, do you, Peter?" she purred.

"No, no," he gulped.

Her hand cracked against his buttocks, hard.

"Mistress!" he gasped.

"Don't forget again, boy."

"I-I'm sorry, mistress," he panted, raising and lowering himself.

"Turn around."

He turned on the bar, lifting himself up, working his already aching muscles.

"Stop. Hold yourself there."

He froze in place, his chin at the bar, his arms starting to throb.

Then his eyes widened as he felt her lips against his cock. His pulse pounded and he cringed, trying to restrain his excitement as her lips slid further and further down his cock, as he felt more and more of his throbbing erection slide between her lips, over her tongue and...

Down her throat!

He was so shocked as he felt himself going into her throat that he could not react. He felt her lips wrap around the very base of his cock, and then slide quickly back and forth up and down his throbbing shaft. His body tensed, close now to his peak, Kathleen sensed it and withdrew.

He came, spurting his seed out onto the floor, as she moved aside, squeezing his cock and laughing up at him as he groaned and gasped, spurting again and again. He fell down and she stepped back with a smirk.

"Dirty boy," Kathleen said. "You leave a mess everywhere you go."

He panted weakly, legs rubbery, then fell back to his knees.

She stepped in front of him, and then slowly eased her short, tight skirt up her thighs to reveal a tiny black V of lacy material over her groin. She half turned, and he inhaled sharply, seeing her bared buttocks and the neat little slash of black sliding up between them. She slipped her thumbs into the sides of her thong and eased it down, then half turned again, holding the thong in her hands.

Her pussy was naked. And he gaped at sight of it, at how lewdly bare it was, how neat and luscious the little slash was, excited by the very idea that she had removed all her pubic hair. He stared at it in dazed fascination, but when his hands came up she slapped them down, then slid the thong over his head, pulling it down around his throat and then tightening her grip on the material to pull him into her groin.

"Lick me," she ordered.

He obeyed, moaning into her groin, licking awkwardly at first then lapping hungrily at her sex in a fervent hunger as she mashed his face against her. Then, as some semblance of control returned to him, he began to tongue her with more expertise. Yet she was not impressed.

"You lick like a dog," she sniffed. "Didn't you ever learn the most basic of techniques? I had better lickings when I was sixteen from girlfriends during sleepovers."

His cock throbbed and twitched at the thought of a young Kathleen with her nubile young girlfriends, naked in a bed. He raised his hands and clutched her buttocks, but she twisted her fingers in his hair until he cried out in pain and dropped them to his sides again. Then she began to instruct him on how she wanted her sex attended to, where and how to lick, and with what strength, how often and how deep she expected his tongue to slide up inside her, how fast and with what pressure his lips should work against her clitoris.

When she came it was with a slight shudder, a fluttering of her eyes, and a harsh grinding motion as her hands drew his face in more powerfully. Then she exhaled deeply and stepped back.

"You'll do better in future," she said, lowering her skirt.

She pulled him to his feet and slapped his bottom.

"Back to the office, slut."

***

Kathleen honked in irritation as an oversized Bentley pulled in front of her. After pulling ahead and turning into her lane the black car rolled serenely along at a moderate pace, utterly ignoring her as she glared at it impatiently.

"Arrogant bastard," she muttered.

She could not pass it on the left, for a slow lorry kept pace with the Bentley there, and there was traffic to her right. So she fumed, glowering, constantly looking behind and ahead of her for a chance to pass. Finally, a space opened and she shoved her foot to the floor. The Ford shot ahead into the wrong lane and accelerated past the Bentley. She turned long enough to see a distinguished looking man with salt and pepper hair look down his nose at her from behind the wheel of the Bentley, then cut just in front of him, forcing him to stand on his brakes.

She laughed as she looked into the rear view mirror, and then held her hand out of the window to wave nonchalantly.

Upper class bastard. Rich, satisfied, arrogant. Probably inherited every pound he had and used his connections to keep from going bankrupt. Snotty, superior windbag. They were all like that, all thinking they were better than anyone else merely because their ancestors, somewhere along the line, had been lucky and made money.

No one had gifted Kathleen Hunter with anything when she was born. She was born into poverty in the East End, and grew up in council housing with an alcoholic mother. She had no idea who her father had been, nor, she suspected, did her mother. Kathleen had scrambled for everything she had ever had, and only after puberty, when her looks had begun turning heads and she had discovered how to manipulate men, had she begun to pull out of that miserable life.

First she had flirted with male teachers, which had helped her grades somewhat. Letting them paw at her body had done even better, and then she had given herself to several, as well as her headmaster, and thus had "earned" marks sufficient to bring her a scholarship to a small, moderately respected college. There she had continued her efforts, for though she was cunning and smart she could not match the intelligence and sheer diligence of some of the other students. The Asians, in particular, thought nothing of spending all evening and every evening in study, often surviving on three or four hours sleep night after night. She could not live like that. She found she hated studies, and was not very good at examinations. She was quite good, intuitively, in software design, but the rigidly structured examination formulas, asking absurd questions about little-known commands made this impossible.

Nevertheless, she got top marks. Almost all her masters were male, and almost all of them, having spent a lifetime in software design, were nerdy, geeky, and regarded flattering attention from a beautiful woman with open-mouthed astonishment. They were so easy to manipulate it was hardly even a challenge.

Her classmates were something else again. The pampered children of the upper classes, or at least, the upper middle class. They took money for granted. They had nice cars and talked casually about their vacations in America and Italy and Spain. The men spoke like pansies; snotty snobbish idiots, all of them. The women were lazy bitches, used to being looked after, and sure that that would continue. The men were grunting pigs, desperate to please.

Almost all men were fools; weak, stupid, undignified animals that could be twisted and turned any way a beautiful woman desired. Kathleen found a great deal of pleasure in that, not merely in manipulating them, but in persuading them to humiliate themselves, to demean themselves before her for no better reason than she was reasonably good looking.

She thought about Peter and smiled to herself. Such a cute boy, and so good at his work too. She had plans for Peter, big plans. She had no intention of spending her life in miserable toil in a sanitised office building in London. Kathleen did not like working. She did not like being forced to keep to a schedule, to plan her life around the demands of an institution. Spending more than half her waking life at a keyboard, or worse, in meetings with fools, was better than living life as her mother did, but didn't hold a candle to her ambitions.

SpecterWare was a small, little-known company that had been plodding along for some years, ekeing out a small profit sometimes, other years losing money. Its stock went for slightly over a pound on the London Stock Exchange, but languished, barely moving from year to year. Few analysts paid any attention to the company. Most had never heard of it.

It was perfect.

She had persuaded its Board of Directors to appoint her head of software development through the simple expediency of sleeping with three of its members, and blackmailing two others, one of whom had a mistress and the other a drug habit. Then, through similar means, she had gained a loan, ostensibly for the company, from a "friendly" banker. The loan was only fifty thousand pounds, hardly enough to draw scrutiny.

She had used this to purchase stock options in SpecterWare. The way options worked was that she need only put up ten percent of the present day cost of the stock she purchased. She then owned that stock, with a set amount of time to pay off the other ninety percent. If the stock went up, she stood to make a good deal of money. If the stock went down, however, she stood to lose a fortune.

She "owned" a half million shares in SpecterWare now. But the shares were priced at half a million pounds. She had put up just fifty, none of which was really hers to begin with. If the stock dropped as much as ten percent she would be out that fifty thousand, and eventually have to explain where it had gone.

Ahh, but if the stock rose!

Many high-technology companies had seen their stock prices go through the roof of late, doubling, tripling, quadrupling, and more. Several had gone up by ten or fifteen times their price in a single year. If she could double the stock price of SpecterWare, her half million pounds of stock would be worth a million pounds - less the cost of actually paying for them, which would still leave her with half a million pounds.

She was more ambitious than that, however. She planned to raise the price of SpecterWare tenfold within six months. That would give her four and a half million pounds, enough to retire on.

She smiled at that. After three years at university and then five years working her way through the industry she was just shy of thirty. If this plan went well she'd be retired by her thirtieth birthday. The best part was that it was all legal - well, except for misappropriating the original loan. But if she paid that back in time no one would be any the wiser.

And, of course, the actions she was going to need to take to raise SpecterWare's profile and stock price were far from legal.

Fortunately, she had many willing helpers. Peter would be one. Charles another. But there would be more, some more willing than others, of course.

CHAPTER THREE

Kathleen pulled to the pavement and parked, then got out and walked up the narrow path to her little rented townhouse. She let herself in, then went up the stairs to her bedroom and casually stripped before donning a leather thong and matching bra. She pulled on a pair of black leather shoes with stiletto heels, then a pair of kid gloves, which extended almost all the way to her shoulders. She pulled her short hair back tautly and fastened it behind her head, then rouged her cheeks, put on a thick layer of dark red lipstick, a bit too much black mascara, and headed downstairs. Silly, in a way, but the effect was often quite favourable on certain types of men.

The clock chimed and she glanced at it. It was made to look like an antique pendulum clock, sitting there on the table, but it was not a thing of carved wood and glass, just cheap plastic she'd bought at a department store. Some day, soon, she would be able to buy the real thing. She'd have a large, beautiful home with grandfather clocks on the landings and thick rugs on the floors. She had champagne tastes, her mother had often told her, but for the moment it was simply beer and pocket money.

She trotted down the narrow stairs, then rounded the corner and unbolted the door to the cellar. She'd specifically chosen this townhouse for its cellar. She couldn't really afford its rent, and in fact, in another two months her store of carefully saved money would run out unless she borrowed more, and she'd be unable to pay at all. Hopefully, by then, it wouldn't matter.

The staircase was quite steep and narrow, and she gripped the rail as she carefully made her way down on her high heels. She felt a bit like a cartoon character in the "costume" and yet, at the same time felt a sense of power and sexual thrill. She knew precisely how men reacted to her when they saw her like this, and smiled with grim anticipation as she reached the bottom step.

She picked up a narrow leather crop where she had left it on a table and then flicked on the lights.

The cellar was quite old, the walls of ancient mortared stone. The floor was bare concrete. The roof was low, heavily limed and supported by soot-darkened wooden beams. In the far corner was a low wooden platform, deep in the shadow of a wide stone pillar. As she rounded the pillar a man came into view. He knelt on the pillar, trembling slightly.

The man was hooded. His mouth was wide, his lips wrapped around an artificial penis which projected from the end of a metal pole just in front of his body. A strap went from the post, around his head, and back again, preventing him from removing his mouth. A thick, rubberised dildo thrust up from beneath him, and was buried deep within his anus. His arms were bound tightly back together behind him, elbows touching. His feet were lifted up and back, pressed against his thighs just below his buttocks, and bound to his wrists.

A metal ring was clamped about his penis just above his testicles, connected by a wire to the post before him, pulled taut. Several elastic bands were wrapped tightly about the shaft of his penis from below the head to the metal ring. His cock was purplish-red and half-erect. Hearing her, he trembled and moaned weakly.

"Hello Charles. Been having a pleasant day?" she asked.

He moaned and trembled again and she chuckled cruelly.

He had a quite good body, for she had owned him for some months now, and had him on a stringent exercise schedule. His pectoral muscles were strongly defined, his stomach flat and lined with muscle. His buttocks were tight and taut; his legs and arm muscles full and powerful.

But he was weak, she thought, as they all were.

She removed his hood, and his blue eyes stared up at her, filled with pain, beseeching her to release him. She slapped his face instead.

"Have you been thinking about me, dog?"

He moaned and tried to nod.

Forty years old, Charles Evans-Finch was a well-respected analyst for one of the City's most powerful brokers. When he began advising his clients to buy SpecterWare stock people would take notice. Some people would buy on reflex, which would make him look good and give the stock momentum. Then a series of well-planned publicity events, some startlingly innovative new products, and she would be on her way to becoming a wealthy woman.

She moved behind him and studied his pain-wracked form, smiling. She saw his cock was now fully erect, or as erect as it could be within the tight grips of the elastic bands. They were cutting deeply into his flesh now, but the pain only served to make him more aroused. She laid the tip of the crop against the small of his back, then trailed it downwards to where the dildo impaled him, rubbing at his flesh were it gripped the plastic.

"Would you like a few more inches inside you, Charles?" she asked tauntingly.

He moaned again and she laughed, and then struck at him lightly, just next to the dildo. He moaned and quivered, jerking on the dildo, pulling against the wire holding his penis in place.

He was not being punished. In fact, he had begged to be given this "challenge", that, at its end, he might be rewarded by being used by her. Kathleen did not often let her men use her sexually. It was not that the feel of a male penis inside her was altogether unpleasant, nor that she was disgusted by the thought. Rather, she knew that rationing it only made sex with her more desperately desired by them.

His shoulders, she knew, would be aching ferociously after twelve hours in that position. He would feel half-crippled for days now. His knees would be worse, for in spite of the strip of padded carpet below them he had all his weight on them. His jaw would ache, as well. In truth, he would be good for nothing for some time to come. She toyed with the idea of cutting him loose, then moving away and getting down on all fours, challenging him to mount her then or never. Would he be able to claw his way across the floor to her? She rather doubted it.

But for now, best not to overdo things.

She unclipped the strap from behind his head and gently pushed his head back, working his lips back off the dildo. He gasped loudly as they came free, and then cried out in pain as his jaw, frozen in place for so long, started to close.

"Move your jaw very, very slowly," she said. "Let it close only slowly and don't try to talk."

He moaned and whimpered, but obeyed.

She removed the wire from the clip attached to his cock, and then depressed a lever that let the dildo slide back into the frame. He cried out and fell back onto his arms. This produced another cry of pain and Kathleen smiled.

She stepped forward, squatted, and roughly rolled him onto his belly. Her fingers unfastened the straps binding his arms together, and he cried out again, loudly. Moments later she released his ankles from their bondage so that he could now straighten his legs.

She stood up and watched him writhe, watched him convulse in pain as cramped arms, shoulders back and legs were at last freed of their confinement. She stepped back as his bent legs slowly, slowly unfurled amid much moaning, groaning and hissing. His arms were flat at his sides, trembling and jerking spastically, and his mouth was wide as he whimpered in pain.

Kathleen felt a tremendous wave of power as she stood above him, watching him writhe and twist helplessly. Her groin grew heavy and warm and after a moment she stripped off her bra and thong, standing straight-legged over him, legs apart, arrogantly smiling down at his torment.

She judged her moment, when the agony of newly released muscles began to give way to the ecstasy of relief, and dropped down upon him. With quick hands she removed the ring from his cock then roughly stripped off the elastics, ignoring his moans of pain.

"Do you want me, dog?" she whispered, straddling him.

He moaned piteously.

She held the head of his cock against her, rubbing it lightly up and down against the lips of her sex. "Do you want me?"

"...eeeeessss," he gasped, shuddering.

She smiled and dropped down slowly. He groaned loudly, his back arching weakly as she took him deeper and deeper into the tightness of her belly. He lay spread-eagled on the cold stone, barely able to move his arms or legs, panting and gasping and whimpering in pleasure now as he felt his cock slip through the hot moist silk of her pussy.

Her gloved hands slid along his chest, and then she dropped fully atop him, grinding herself against his loins, squeezing her pubic muscles around his long-tortured cock. She leaned forward, pressing her soft, full breasts against his chest, letting them pillow out beneath her as she rolled her body from side to side. She slid upwards, letting her breasts dangle over his face, and his arms twitched as he tried to raise them. He halted in pain, gasping, and she smirked, letting her nipples caress his forehead and cheeks. He whimpered every time his mouth moved yet when she let one nipple push against it he closed his lips around it, heedless of the pain, suckling desperately.

"Such a sweet boy," she cooed.

She began to ride him, her buttocks rising smoothly up and down, hips rolling as she twisted from side to side. His body shuddered and trembled beneath her, and he came, his hot semen gushing up into her body. Her tight pussy milked him of every drop, and she continued to rise and fall. His cock, so long mistreated, remained stiff, the flesh exquisitely sensitive, and he continued to moan in a mixture of pleasure and pain, sucking voraciously at her breasts whenever she let one slide against his mouth.

She came herself, glorying in her power over him, in her conquest, in being able to use and abuse him as she wished, in being the subject of such helpless, pathetic devotion. It made her feel astonishingly powerful and seductive, and her insides exulted in the feel of his cock slicing through the soft, elastic flesh of her pussy as she continued to ride him cruelly.

She slapped his face, then backhanded him, then gripped his head and jammed her lips down against his own, tasting blood as her tongue shot into his mouth. He moaned and whimpered, his tongue pushing weakly up against hers. Her thighs clutched his hips and her backside rose and fell, rose and fell, her pussy swallowing almost the entire length of his purplish staff with every drop, pulling upwards and almost off, and then dropping down once more.

He came again, gurgling in ecstasy, and she let her pussy milk the last drop out of him before slowing, kissing him lightly on the forehead, then easing up his body to straddle his face.

Despite the agony of his sore jaw, his lips and tongue moved against her, frantic to please, licking and sucking and tonguing her as he had been instructed, bringing her to yet another orgasm. And then she slid back and mounted him again, for he was hard once more.

When finally she stepped off he lay as he had when she had straddled him, spread-eagled, trembling, slack-jawed, and whimpering, yet now exhausted and barely conscious. She smiled as his eyes closed and he fell asleep, then turned and climbed the stairs, headed for a bath. It had been a long day of work, and she had more like it ahead of her before her goal would be accomplished.

***

The security guard allowed Peter entry on Saturday morning, apparently unconcerned about what he was doing there on a weekend, and not at all suspicious about what perverse sexual games he might be intending to engage in. Peter hurried up to the office, let himself in, and then went to his cubicle. There he tried quite hard to ignore the thought of Kathleen's beauty and strength and make progress on the task she'd set him.

After a few hours he had managed to make some progress, and broke for lunch with a little less worry about what Kathleen would think of him. He had just started back to work when the sound of the outer door drew his head snapping up. He felt a wave of excitement, and an almost instant erection pushed out against his trousers.

He stood up and turned to the cubicle entrance, breathless as he waited. Then she was there, dressed in a short knitted dress, hair pulled tightly back from her forehead, legs looking incredibly long and shapely.

"Well, Peter. And how have you been doing today?"

Peter looked down, blushing. "Not very well."

"Still distracted?"

Peter looked up, grinning in a bashful way which seldom failed to please women.

"Thinking about you," he said.

"Thinking about pleasing me?"

"Yes!"

"Then you should have been working at this project. That would have pleased me."

She pushed him back and looked at what he had done, lips pursed.

"Well, at least it's something," she said grudgingly.

"I'll finish it on time," he promised.

"I think you need more exercise. Come with me to the gym. You could use a break. In fact, I'm thinking of ordering all employees to become involved in a regular fitness program."

"Oh but I..."

"No excuses. Come."

"But I can't - exercise in this!" Peter protested weakly, indicating his tight dress pants and silk shirt.

"Then you can exercise in the nude again," Kathleen said with a smile.

"But what about the security guard? What if..."

"Let me worry about the security guard," she said, glaring now. "Do as you're told."

Biting his lip, Peter followed her down the hall then across the rotunda to the gym.

"Strip," she ordered.

She folded her arms below her breasts and watched as he fumbled at his shirt buttons, then pulled his shirt off. Blushing, he undid his trousers and skinned them off, standing in black string bikini under-shorts. He had bought them from a catalogue years ago, but had rarely worn them.

"Leave those on for a bit," she said.

He nodded obedience and removed his socks and shoes, then stood, quivering with anticipation.

"Do some more chin-ups," Kathleen ordered, pointing to the bar.

He padded across the carpet and reached above him to the bar, then closed his fingers around it and pulled himself up. Kathleen stood before him, studying the play of muscles beneath his skin as he pulled himself up and down, admiring the sight of him hanging by his hands. She thought of how pretty he would look when he was hanging by his wrists instead.

When he could do no more she had him sit on another machine. This one had him spread his legs widely, placed on padded arms, which he must swing in and out to strengthen thigh muscles. At the same time his arms were raised up and out to either side, in another set of padded arms, pulling them in and out.

Kathleen waited a moment, then moved forward, gripped the front of his string bikini shorts and tore them off.

"Very nice," she said admiringly.

His stiff cock thrust out at her hungrily, but she stepped back and motioned for him to continue to exercise.

When he could hardly move them she permitted him to stop, then led him across the floor and through a door marked Ladies Locker Room. Inside to the left was a wide, brown tiled area with showerheads sprouting from one wall. To the right was a toilet lined with cubicles, and between them, a changing room lined with lockers.

Stairs led up from the changing room to a whirlpool bath that was about five metres wide. A small wooden shelf went around it, and more stairs led down the far side into the shower room.

"Arch your back. Pull your head back."

Peter obeyed, feeling his stomach flutter and twist.

His cock twitched as she moved towards him, and he gasped as she reached out and slid a hand over his chest, and then caressed his stomach before reaching down to squeeze his erection.

She moved back after a moment and smiled.

"Put your hands behind your head. Arch your back again. Nice. Now turn to the wall and spread your legs. Bend forwards a little. Ahh, yes. Lovely."

He blushed, then hissed in pleasure as her hand cupped his buttocks, kneading his backside, then caressing the skin. She moved in behind him, and he felt her breasts pressing into his back as her arms went around him. Her hands stroked his belly, then moved down to squeeze and lightly stroke his cock.

He groaned helplessly, body afire with lust and excitement.

"Would you like to fuck me, Peter?" she whispered.

"Yes! God, yes!" he groaned.

She gripped his hair and yanked his head back.

"Mistress," she snarled.

"Yes, mistress! I'm sorry, mistress!" he cried.

She slapped her hand down against his buttocks, squeezing and kneading his flesh before stepping back.

"Turn around," she ordered.

He turned and she tossed him a bar of soap. "Turn on the water and soap yourself up. No, not your chest," she said with a smirk.

Peter swallowed repeatedly, then soaped up his groin, his fingers slipping through the soap as he stroked his cock. The water spattered down around him, and he stepped forward, grinning at Kathleen as he worked up a good lather. He dropped the soap, giving her a cocky look, still stroking himself as she looked on.

"Close your eyes, you little slut, and tell me how much you want to stick that soapy cock of yours into me."

He trembled weakly, but obeyed, closing his eyes, standing before her, stroking his hands back and forth as he groaned in pleasure.

"I-I want to fuck you," he panted.

"How, big boy?"

"On all fours," he said. "Like a bitch in heat."

"That's not going to happen. Think of another position."

"I-I'd like to spread your legs and slide between them, and..."

"Think of something else."

His hands slid back and forth along his cock, and he trembled with excitement.

"I'd like to lay back and have you climb over me," he

whispered. "And use me like a... a..."

"Cheap toy?"

"Yes," he moaned.

"Now open your eyes."

He opened his eyes, hoping and almost expecting to see her naked. Instead he saw her standing, fully clothed, next to a strange woman, a black woman. The woman was tall, even taller than Kathleen, her face haughty, aristocratic, her body powerful and muscular, sleek, the skin gleaming, and her eyes, deadly, cold, fixed on Peter's own wide, shocked face as she smirked in contempt.

"This is Yvette," Kathleen said.

"You'll pardon me if I don't shake hands," Yvette said scathingly.

Peter could only stare, horrified, his hands frozen around his soapy cock as soapsuds trickled down his bare legs.

"Well, he does have a nice sized cock," Yvette said casually.

"Yes, but his body could use some work. I'm going to have to get him exercising more."

Peter felt himself getting dizzy and realised he had stopped breathing. He inhaled deeply and staggered back against the wall, the water from the tap now pouring down over him as the two women looked on.

"Clumsy boy though," Yvette said.

Kathleen nodded. "Discipline. He needs discipline."

Yvette was wearing a black blazer, trousers, and a white blouse. She shrugged off the blazer, tossing it to Kathleen, and then peeled her blouse up and off and undid her trousers. Moments later she stood naked, her back ramrod straight as she padded forward like a leopard. A powerful leopard. Her arms and legs were thicker than Peter's, her shoulders were broader as well. She was the most muscular woman Peter had ever seen, almost mannish in the size of her muscles. Her cornrows dangled down to her hips, however, as she stood before him, and Peter found that while his erection had faded during his initial shock, it was starting to rise once again.

"Do you think you're man enough for me, child?" she demanded, her voice deep and thick.

Her hand, an enormous hand, slid up under his jaw, fingers going halfway around his head as she forced him to his toes, then turned him around and back towards a long bench. He gasped as the edge of the bench hit the backs of his heels and gripped her arm as he began to fall. She smiled, lowering him gently onto his back along the narrow bench, then straddling it and looking down at him.

He looked up, awed, frightened, and excited as she straddled him. He saw she, like Kathleen, had no pubic hair and her cleft dropped lower and lower as she slowly settled herself over his groin.

She smirked at him, taking his cock, now rinsed free of soap and rubbing it along her abdomen. "Have you ever been used by a black woman, child?"

He shook his head dumbly and she smiled anew.

She raised herself up on powerful legs, rubbed the head of his thick cock back and forth along her bare slit, then sank down over him, enveloping him, surrounding him, squeezing him powerfully with her internal muscles until she had taken him in all the way.

He reached up for her breasts with trembling hands, and she tolerated his touch for long seconds before gripping his wrists and shoving them back forcefully to the bench above his head. Then she began to ride him, dark, flinty eyes boring into his own as her hips worked up and down.

"Beg for it, child," she ordered. "Beg for mamma to give you what you want."

"F-fuck me," he panted. "Please, mistress. Fuck me like a dog, like a... a cheap toy."

His voice trailed off into a long groan as she rode faster, her hands sliding off his wrists, then down his body. Abruptly her head shot down; her mouth open and her tongue out like a striking snake. Her lips crushed his and her tongue drove deep into his mouth. He moaned and writhed, his arms going around her as one of her hands gripped his hair and forced his head up. He felt his lips bruise as her tongue swept through his mouth with voracious force. Her hips continued to rise and fall as she rode his stiff prick, and he whimpered beneath her, lost in the strength of his excitement and the excitement of her strength.

"Oh God! Oh yes!" he moaned. "Yes! Yes! Ohhhh!"

"Filthy little boy," she growled.

Her lips darted in again and this time he cried out as her teeth bit into the nape of his neck.

"You shall be my slut," she growled, head rising again, face fierce as her hips ground against him. "I will use you to masturbate."

She rode faster, and still faster, her hips a blur as her muscled thighs drove her against him. He grunted and gasped as her groin slammed down against him repeatedly, crushing him into the hard wooden bench. She was irresistible, like a force of nature, like a wild animal, a wild leopard. He was helpless beneath her, and could only lay there, dazed and moaning as she used him in precisely the manner she described.

"You must stay hard, my little dildo," she said, glaring warningly. "I like my masturbation to last."

He quivered, and fought against the excitement sizzling through his veins. He wasn't at all sure how long he could hold back with a wild woman like this riding his cock. Her insides were squeezing and clasping his shaft every time she pulled up, and it took every ounce of will power to keep from exploding within her.

He turned his head away, unable to meet that powerful gaze any longer, and looked into Kathleen's eyes. She stood against the wall, leaning back, watching with a casual but contemptuous smile on her face, and he felt a wave of shame mingled with elation. And then he came despite himself, bucking up against the wild black woman as she cursed and slapped him and rode harder still.

"You miserable slut!" she snarled. "You better not get soft. I'm not through masturbating yet!"

"These untrained men are good for nothing," Kathleen said.

"Then train him. Discipline him."

"Yes, I think we can do that."

Yvette stood up, glaring angrily, and his softening cock slipped out of her. She grabbed him and yanked him up, then as Kathleen opened the door, marched him out into the exercise room.

Peter looked nervously at the closed door to the rotunda, and then grunted as Yvette led him over to one of the machines. It was the one he had used earlier, sitting in its seat and reaching up above to pull the weighted arms in and out. Except now Yvette pushed him face first against it, and to his astonishment, and then intense excitement, Kathleen produced small, soft lengths of cord, lifting his right hand up to one of the bars and tying his wrist there. Yvette did the same with his other hand, and he found himself forced to bend forward as the seat pushed into his belly.

"Wh-what are you doing?" he gulped nervously.

"Punishing you, slut," Kathleen said firmly.

The two women stood back and Peter looked up at his bound wrists in wonder. He pulled against the cord experimentally, then turned his head around to look at the two women.

"Weak men must be disciplined," Yvette said coolly.

His cock began to twitch and harden.

Kathleen had his belt in her hand, the belt from his pants, looped in two with the buckle in her hand.

"Are you sorry for being such a poor excuse for a sex toy?" she demanded mockingly.

"Yes," he breathed.

"Say it then."

"I-I..." He inhaled deeply. "I'm sorry for getting soft, mistress. I'm sorry for not being a good er, sex toy for..."

Crack!

"Unghg!"

The belt whipped down against his buttocks with painful force, and his belly was jammed against the seat.

"Filthy little man," Yvette snapped excitedly.

Crack!

"Christ!" he uttered in pain.

The belt struck again and he cried out, jerking against the cords, his body twisting helplessly.

"Is your little bottom getting sore, Peter?" Kathleen asked tauntingly.

"I thought schoolboys were supposed to be used to having their bottoms spanked," Yvette said.

"He's such a sissy," Kathleen sighed in disappointment.

Crack! Crack! Crack! Crack!

Peter groaned and twisted, but tried to keep silent as the belt continued to strike his buttocks. The pain mounted, the heat growing stronger until his entire backside felt as though it was on fire. Yet he dared not complain. What kind of a weakling could not take something as mild as this? Why, there was a time when schoolboys were caned for infractions, and this wasn't nearly as bad as -

Crack!

"Agghh!" he uttered.

The belt had surprised him by landing across his lower

back. His head whipped around as the belt landed again, this time across his shoulders.

God, they were bitches! Cunning, vicious, brutal, sexy, gorgeous bitches! And they were whipping him! Unbelievably, he was being whipped; bound, naked, and whipped!

Crack!

He arched his back, pulling against the cords, fighting the pain even as his cock began to harden once again. They were whipping him like a slave on a plantation! And he felt a dark inner fire screaming up through his nerves and sinews, through bone and blood and flesh at the understanding that he was theirs to do with as they chose, to beat and abuse, to use for their pleasure. He was a prisoner to these beautiful, powerful women, and as the belt slashed across his back again he felt a strange exultation at the pain which swept over him.

The belt slashed across his back again and he gasped with pain and pleasure, feeling a strange sense of elation, of martyrdom and sacrifice and lust.

Yvette moved beside him and her hand slipped down between his legs, squeezing his cock.

"Are you ready to work again, little dildo?"

"Yes, mistress" he groaned.

She smirked, and then moved around him, slipping into the seat, slumping to its edge, and wrapping her long legs around his thighs as she pulled him into her. He groaned in delight as he thrust into her, and stared and then cried out as Kathleen brought the belt down across his back again.

"Go on, you worthless piece of shit. Fuck her!" she ordered.

The belt lashed across his backside and he yelped as he thrust forward, burying himself in Yvette's hot depths.

"Faster, you dog!"

Crack!

He moaned and shuddered, thrusting faster and faster into

Yvette's pussy as Kathleen continued to bring the belt whipping down across his lower back and buttocks. The sharp flashes of pain exploded amidst the hot, steaming pleasure growing within him, hurling it higher and higher. He spread his legs wider to lower his body and let him thrust more deeply into Yvette, ignoring the pain as the cords cut more deeply into his wrists.

Yvette slumped lower, her eyes closed, groaning. Her legs were still around him, jerking him against her body in time to his thrusts. Her finger stroked her clitoris as she began to writhe and twist in pleasure, and soon she was panting for breath as the heat took hold of her.

He thrust faster, his hips grinding and rolling as he watched his thick cock disappear between the tight, clutching lips of her sex, watched the beautiful, powerful woman's face given over to the pleasure she was taking from him. Each time the belt landed it sent a shock of sensation through his body, with the effect of throwing paraffin onto a fire. He felt a madness grip him, a madness of pleasure, of wildfire sexual heat and lust.

Kathleen rained blows down on him, and the world narrowed to that hot, burning pussy wrapped around his cock, the heat of his tortured flesh and the incredible sexual maelstrom gripping his mind and body. Yvette came, and her pussy clamped down around his pistoning cock like a hard fist, squeezing and pulling at it as his own orgasm arrived. Convulsions racked his body and he cried out, throwing his head back, rutting blindly as the belt continued to snap against his aching flesh.

CHAPTER FOUR

Charles Evans-Finch had built up, over time, a reputation as an astute analyst of the high-technology sector. He had made billions of dollars for his employers, the ALG group, who administered corporate and private investments as well as a variety of mutual funds. In addition, he had been building a reputation in the investment community at large. When Charles Evans-Finch issued pronouncements on this or that company or sector, people listened, and a good many of them acted upon what he said. He had a keen eye for the bottom line, for future growth prospects, and for spotting companies, which were on the edge of major changes.

There were few, looking at the history of SpecterWare, who would have predicted such for them. None, in fact. The company was in a stable area of technology, but stability meant predictability. There were not going to be any massive increases in sales from them, not in that area, so there was no reason whatever to expect an increase in their stock price.

He could not simply start out by telling people to buy the stock, not without justifications he could not give. What he could do was hint, in his newsletter, a newsletter some of the most influential brokers in the UK subscribed to, that major changes were in the works. Something exciting and new which would shake up the company, and more importantly, their profitability. He would be mysterious, at first, and merely advise people to "keep an eye" on the company.

That would almost certainly raise the stock's price as some people bought, speculating that he must have inside information. This would please those who held the stock, mainly pension fund managers who needed stability, and make him look good, at least to those who bought it immediately. Because most of the stockholders were pension fund managers the stock should hold onto that new price for a while. There would be few selling out to take quick profits. And SpecterWare would now be seen as a stock on the move.

But there would have to be more than that, much more. Not even he could really affect a stock's price in the long-term, not by the numbers Mistress wanted. He had advised her of exactly what she must do to make SpecterWare a high flyer - if only temporarily, of how she could raise the company's stock price through momentum and the bidding of fools who spent little effort on research. Mistress wanted to be wealthy, and deserved to be wealthy. This would make her so.

He thought of her as Mistress, even when alone, Mistress. He trembled slightly at her remembered image, so strong, so powerful, so arrogant and proud and beautiful. The world should grovel before her, yet only he had the right.

What he was doing was dangerous, to his reputation, to his financial health, even to his freedom. But if Mistress wanted it he was prepared to face that danger.

He put the finishing touches to his carefully worded notice, and then sent it out to subscribers.

***

Peter could hardly wait to get to work the next day and see Kathleen. He was among the first to arrive and, after going to his cubicle, he casually took a sheaf of printouts and went to Kathleen's office, knocking respectfully.

"Enter."

He walked in, closing the door behind him, and was almost struck dumb by her beauty.

"Come here, Peter," she ordered.

He hurried forward, placing the printouts on her desk.

"On your knees, slut."

Thrilled, he obeyed at once, his heart pounding, his cock beginning to stiffen.

"At the end of the week you're going to quit SpecterWare."

Peter blinked at her in surprise.

"You're going to go and work for Jentech technologies."

"I am?" he asked in confusion.

"Yes, I've arranged it through a personnel placement agency. They'll want to interview you first, of course. But you're exactly what they're looking for."

"Y-you mean I wouldn't work here any longer?"

"That's right."

"But why?" he exclaimed. "Is it because I was late with the - "

"No, silly boy. It's because Jentech is working on an innovative way to add a degree of artificial intelligence logic to computerised order entry systems. It will revolutionise the entire sector. I want you to steal everything you can on it and send it to me."

He stared at her, appalled. "But I can't do that!"

She smiled. "Of course you can."

"I mean, I could go to jail for that!"

"Oh, not very likely, and you need fear that only if you get caught."

He stood up slowly. "Kathleen, I can't!"

She slapped his face and he staggered back, giving her a wounded look.

"Don't tell me you can't, boy."

"But I..."

Kathleen picked up a remote control and turned on a television in the corner. Peter turned and stared, appalled, at the sight of him bent over the stool. There was no sign of Kathleen except her legs, but his own body was perfectly displayed. He watched the paddle coming down on his backside, and heard himself cry out for more. He watched himself spurt his semen onto the rug, and then a quick scene change showed him in the locker room of the gym, as Yvette rode him and he begged to be her sex toy, her dildo.

He felt sick.

"Peter, Peter, Peter," she cooed, moving forward to slide her arms around him. "I'm only showing you this so you know you have no choice. You don't want your friends seeing these, do you, or mummy and daddy?"

He stared at her, shocked.

'No, of course you don't,' she said, smiling tolerantly. "You're going to enjoy our little game of espionage, aren't you, and so much more."

She pushed him back and he watched her calmly reach down to the hem of her short, tight dress. She slid the hem up slowly, baring her thighs, then her pantieless groin, then pulled it off over her head. Naked, she was magnificent, and he could only gape at her.

Her breasts were large, as he'd imagined, but incredibly firm for their size, with perfect round nipples in the exact centre of each. She had a slim stomach, flat, with barely discernible muscle just beneath the surface. Her hips were round and womanly, and her thighs alone could have made him erect, so perfect were their contours. She was a goddess, and he dropped to his knees again, without even being told

She smiled and moved towards him, gripping his head, then sliding her hands behind it as she pulled him back to his feet. She pressed her naked breasts into his chest and kissed him deeply.

He moaned, his mind spinning, and then gasped as her hand slid between his legs and began to squeeze his manhood. Confusion filled his mind, but his lust was rising higher. She shoved him back so that he half fell into a hard-backed chair then straddled the armless chair and straddled him. She eased lower, letting her naked buttocks slide up his thighs, and she gripped his head in powerful hands, crushing his lips with hers.

He moaned, his tongue like a sparrow against hers - the hawk, small, helpless, battered, overpowered. She pulled back and he gasped, dazed, then she reached down, undid his trousers, and pulled him free.

"Do you want me, you little slut?"

"Yes! Oh yes! Oh God!"

She slapped his face, rocking his head back.

"Mistress," she said calmly.

He blinked against little dots of light in his eyes, then felt her sex against the head of his cock. She slid down over him, enveloping him, drawing him up inside her tight, moist heat, and he could only groan at the wonder of it. She pulled his head forward and jammed his face against her breasts, squeezing them together with her arms, wordlessly commanding him to worship them.

He licked and slurped and suckled madly, his hands coming up, trying to fill themselves with her soft flesh, but she forced them back, pinning them down; eyes boring into his as her hips rose and fell in effortless grace, riding up and down on his quivering body, using him as Yvette had, as her sex toy. He fought desperately to calm himself, to hold back, and the agonising effort was enough to distract him just long enough to see her eyes flutter and feel her insides spasm and pull on his cock. Then he exploded.

He would do whatever Kathleen wanted, but that wasn't such a bad thing. Kathleen wouldn't really hurt him, and he could not bear the thought of abandoning her and going back to his dull, virtuous, boring life.

CHAPTER FIVE

Jeffrey Fitzwilliams was a millionaire. He and his partners had put together a web site consulting business when he was fresh out of university and had gone public a few months later. Now all of them were millionaires and Ecom, their company was poised for even better things. One of his partners had figured out a way to take advantage of the growing speed of internet traffic by using an old technique in digital splicing that would triple Ecom's profits within a year. The best part was that no one else had figured it out. He had given some broad hints to a few very selected analysts who would begin to prepare the market by talking up Ecom's stock, but they were all quite reliable and discreet men. When Ecom announced its new development it would take the Internet world by storm.

He turned off the alarm on his Porsche and unlocked the door, then opened it and bent to get in. Suddenly, a pair of strong hands seized him by the scruff of the neck and hurled him head first into the car so that he wound up sprawled on the passenger side floor. He scrambled to twist around and up but a hard foot rammed into his backside and shoved his face into the rug.

"Stay where you are, sweetie," a female voice ordered.

The car door slammed, the engine started, and the car backed up.

He turned and saw an enormous black woman sitting in the driver's seat.

"Are you mad?" he shouted, trying to get up again.

Again a foot slammed into him, jamming him against the floorboard and held him in place.

"Don't make me angry, little boy," the woman growled dangerously. "You won't like me when I'm angry."

If she had been a man he would likely have heeded her

words. But she was a woman, and everyone knew women were weaker than men. The idea of being afraid of a woman was absurd. What kind of a man would give in to intimidation by a woman and let her steal his car? So Jeffrey tried again to twist around, cursing and snarling as she laughed and used her foot to pin him in place. He was amazed at her strength. Her leg was like a tree trunk, and he could not twist or push it aside.

"Let me go, you stupid bitch!" he screamed in frustration and rage.

"Eventually, little boy. And don't call me names or I'll have to spank you."

"I'll have you in bloody prison!"

"I don't think that's very likely."

She pulled into a garage and stopped, then reached down and caught hold of one of his ankles.

"I think you're being too noisy for a long drive," she said, yanking off his shoe and then his sock.

"What are you doing? Are you mad? Let go of me!" he demanded shrilly.

She chuckled softly, and then she was yanking at his trousers. Mortified, Jeffrey fought to keep hold of them, but she was incredibly strong, and soon had them and his shorts off. Gaping, he tried to cover himself, and she used the distraction to pull off his other shoe, and then yank at his golf shirt.

"Let me go! I'll give you my wallet!"

"Thanks, love. Don't need it."

She yanked off his golf shirt, and then had him across her lap, bare and naked, and was pinning his wrists behind his back. Jeffrey had never been so humiliated in his life. He had never imagined it was possible to be so humiliated. He thought that surely it was possible to die of embarrassment and that if so he was about to do so.

She handcuffed his wrists together, and then yanked on

his hair. When he opened his mouth to scream she stuffed a spongy ball of some kind into his mouth, used a thick, fat finger to force it in deeper, then strapped a bit of leather around his head to hold it in place.

"Nice little bottom you have here, Jeffrey," she said, giving his buttocks a squeeze.

Jeffrey moaned in embarrassment, then squealed as she fondled his genitals.

"But you can spend the rest of the trip in peace and quiet," she said.

She dragged him out of the car, and he stared around him desperately, half relieved, and half in despair at seeing nothing but a dimly lit, empty parking lot. The black woman held his arm, and forced him around to the rear of his car, then opened the boot. It was small, but this apparently did not daunt her. She removed the spare tyre, tossing it onto the pavement behind her, threw out his toolbox and spare jacket, and then squeezed him into it and slammed the hood.

The rest of the trip was indeed quiet, for he heard nothing but the sounds of traffic as he huddled, moaning, terrified, and humiliated in the boot, thinking that he had surely been kidnapped to be held for ransom. The trip was not long, and then the boot was being opened and his bulging eyes looked up at the smiling black woman again.

She dragged him out, and he saw that once again they were in a garage. This was a tiny one car garage of a type attached to individual houses however, and he was dragged through a door, down a short hall and then down a flight of stairs into a dark, dimly lit basement. She bent him over a low table and undid the handcuffs. He tried to pull his arms free, but she held them easily in place, one huge hand pinning his wrists. She then picked up two thick leather restraints, slipping them around his wrists and fastening them tightly.

She pulled his arms straight up above him, clipped the

restraints together, and then slipped them over a hook hanging by a low chain. Jeffrey cried out as the chain rose, and he was lifted to his toes, then off them, to dangle helplessly from his wrists. He felt the pain set into his body as the leather, even while padded, cinched tightly around his slim wrists and then the ache as his arms began to complain at supporting his weight.

The woman stood back, smirking at him, and he stared back, horrified, and then dropped his eyes. He had never felt so utterly exposed, so naked and helpless, nor so... so small.

She removed the strap around his head, and then pulled out the spongy ball. He gasped and worked his jaw, but did not know what to say.

"Such a pretty little boy," she said, reaching forward to grope his genitals.

"Stop that!" he cried.

She chuckled but ignored him. He tried to kick at her and got a clout to the face that had him seeing stars, and then a fist sank deep into his stomach and had him coughing and gasping for breath.

She moved behind him and he cringed as her fingers squeezed and kneaded his buttocks.

"Would you like me to let you go, little man?"

He was still panting for breath and did not answer. She slapped her hand against his buttocks and he yelped, twisting on the chain.

"All you have to do, little man, is give me some information."

"Information?" he gasped.

"Yes, on your new digital splicing technique. I want you to tell me all about it."

He gaped at her, astounded. Of all the things he had feared or imagined, of all the things he had tried to prepare for, this had never even entered his mind.

"You're joking?"

"No, little man. You're going to tell me all about it. You're going to give me the codes and passwords to get into your company's computer, and then, if you're good, I shall let you go."

"I-I can't do that! I won't!"

"Won't?" she said dangerously. "I think I can change your mind, little man."

Without further word she snatched up another pair of restraints, attaching them to the trembling man's ankles then spread his legs wide apart and chained them in place. She wrapped a belt around his waist, and then, humming softly to herself, showed him a narrow metal probe not much thicker than a pencil, and only slightly longer. It was attached to a long wire, which led to a small machine set in the corner.

With a smile, she moved her face against his, reaching around him with beefy arms, squeezing his buttocks. He gasped as he felt her finger press against his rectum.

"Stop it! Don't! No!"

She chuckled as she slowly pushed the probe into his anus, smiling as he writhed and cursed in fear, alarm and embarrassment.

She pushed it deep, then used a small leather strap to pin it to the back of the belt.

"Won't, little man?"

"You're mad! You're insane! They'll lock you up forever!"

"Better watch out then. If I'm insane there's no telling what I'll do."

She depressed a switch and Jeffrey screamed as a shock rippled through his belly.

"Wha-what are..."

She turned a knob and he screamed again, his body trembling. The trembling grew more and more violent as she sent more power through the little probe, and his scream became a warbling wail of agony.

"You dance so nicely, little man," she said, dark eyes hooded. "So prettily."

She turned the knob back down so only a minimal amount of power moved through the wire.

"Shocking, hmmm?" she asked, smiling gently.

Jeffrey continued to tremble violently, his movements gradually subsiding until he went limp, his head hanging forward.

"Now, now, little man. There's no need for you to feel such discomfort," she cooed, squeezing his groin. "We can have fun instead if you like."

She slipped the probe out of his rectum and gave his buttocks a squeeze.

"I just thought you would like to see what awaits you if you displease me," she said. "Of course, if you please me, we could have fun together."

She was kneading his buttocks with one hand. Now the other began to stroke his cock, squeezing and massaging the head as she pressed her breasts against his chest. She sank to her knees, cupping his buttocks with both hands as she took him into her mouth. Her finger pushed against his anus, then probed within, dipping in lightly, circling and stroking.

He moaned weakly, dazed by the bizarre turn which his life had taken, hardly able to credit he was hanging by his wrists naked before an enormous, muscular woman. He cringed as her teeth nibbled lightly at the base of his cock, then cringed again as, against his will, he felt himself begin to harden.

"S-stop it," he begged.

"You'd prefer more electric therapy?" she asked, smiling up at him.

He blanched in fear and she chuckled evilly, and then took him into her mouth again. Her finger pushed deeper into his bottom now, and he squirmed mentally. Disgusted. Yet her finger did not hurt. In fact, much to his surprise, the sensation was not at all unpleasant.

His cock hardened further within her mouth, and he gasped to see her lips slide down its length to the base, to feel the head of his cock slipping over her tongue and down into her very throat. He stared up at the ceiling in despair, trying to control himself, yet he could not. As her lips began to work up and down on his erection and her finger pumped in and out of his rectum he felt a growing sense of excitement, hating himself for it.

She stood up, looking down at him with a smile, and Jeffrey felt both relief and disappointment. Then she took his erection and pushed her hips forward. He gasped as he realised her intentions, staring down as she raised her right leg and half curled it around his body. She pulled his cock against her shaven sex, and he whimpered as he felt the head sink in. Then she thrust her hips forward and swallowed his shaft, her big hands squeezing his buttocks tightly as she pulled herself against him.

"Ahhh, so nice," she whispered, grinding her pelvis lewdly. "See how much fun we can have, little man?"

Her finger pushed into his rectum again, pumping in and out as she worked her hips against him. His head hung back as he panted for breath, and he stared at the ceiling, whimpering, unable to believe what was happening to him.

And yet the pleasure could not be ignored. Much as he feared and hated the horrible woman his body craved the soft heat of her body. He was not...quite... a virgin, but he was close enough to one to find any female contact intensely exciting. Were it not for his physical discomfort, the pain in his wrists and arms, and his fear of what she might do to him - not to mention his indignation and shame at being forced, at being raped by a woman - he would have considered this one of the most exciting events of his life.

He could feel her insides squeezing around his cock, squeezing repeatedly as she worked her pubic muscles, as she pulled her hips in and out. He fought for breath, groaning at the pain in his wrists, yet still the pleasure rose, and with it shame and despair.

"Come inside me, baby boy," she cooed. "Come inside mummy, little man."

And he did, his juices spewing out of his over-excited body as the woman ground herself against him, as her arms squeezed him tightly and her finger pumped quickly in his rectum. He felt his hips trying to work, trying to buck against her, and tears of shame filled his eyes as the woman laughed at him and her body drank up the last drop of his semen.

She stepped back with a smirk, and he dropped his eyes to the floor.

"Won't we have fun together," she said, beaming.

Yvette gave his bottom another squeeze then left the room, leaving him alone. She was not worried about the police. The only dangerous part lay behind her. Once she was done with this little man he would be so humiliated by his experience he would rather die than tell anyone about it. To be kidnapped by a woman was bad enough, but to be tormented, and sexually molested by one, and to enjoy it - which she would see to - would be too much of a blow to his manhood. No, he would not tell the police, nor even his partners. He would tell no one. And when SpecterWare came out with a nearly identical product before his company did, no one would be able to prove a connection.

"Poor Jeffrey. Not feeling well?"

Jeffrey groaned and opened his eyes. He had been hanging by his wrists for what felt like hours. He was exhausted, his wrists and hands numb, his arms burning. He was sweating heavily, and his hair was matted against his skull. He stared at the woman before him in dazed but growing confusion. This was not the big black woman, but another woman entirely. She was tall but blonde, and wore a purple lace cat suit, which did virtually nothing to hide a spectacular figure, or a pair of brown nipples, which were erect, despite the hot, stuffy air.

He flushed red, aware once again of his own nudity.

"Wh-who are you?" he panted.

"You may call me... Mistress."

The blonde woman smiled, then reached down to fondle his groin. She gently massaged his testicles, squeezed his cock, and began to rub the underside of the head with her thumb, all the while smiling brightly at him.

"Jeffrey, you're quite a pretty young man. Has anyone told you that before?"

He looked past her shoulder, too embarrassed to speak.

"Now don't be like that. Some men like to be dominated by women," she said.

"Wha-what are you talking about? I don't like..."

"I think you do," she interrupted, squeezing his cock harder as it began to stiffen.

She reached behind her and the front of her cat suit slipped down, baring a pair of magnificent breasts. Jeffrey could not keep his eyes from leaping towards them, and he inhaled sharply. He had very little experience with women. He had spent his life around computers, and had always been thought of as a geek. Now he was rich, of course, but he still spent ten or twelve hours a day in front of a computer. He knew how to operate computers. He knew very little about how to talk with women.

"P-please don't," he gulped.

She pressed her finger against his lips.

"L-let me down," he gasped.

"You have to ask nicely if you want anything, Jeffrey,"

she said.

Her hand went behind his head and she abruptly leaned forward. Then her lips were against his, her tongue in his mouth, and those wonderful breasts pressed hard against his naked chest. His cock pulsed and thickened in her hand, and she began to stroke her fist up and down its length.

"You want me, don't you, Jeffrey?" she purred.

"Please," he moaned.

"Say it," she whispered. "Say it, Jeffrey."

"I... I want you," he gasped dazedly.

"You're so weak, Jeffrey. But so are all men."

She stepped back and peeled her cat suit down, then arched back, smiling at the hunger in his eyes. Wearing only a G-string and heels, she moved to a low table, and he saw it held a small notebook computer.

"Now, Jeffrey, first we have to do a few things. "What is your user name and password?"

"Wh-why?"

She smiled and stepped back to him, then slapped his face.

"You must remember to say 'mistress,' Jeffrey. It's a sign of respect for your betters."

You rich bastard, she thought.

A small trickle of blood made its way down from the corner of his mouth, and she seized his head between her hands and kissed him, then let her tongue slide over his chin and along his lip, lapping up the blood. She stepped back a foot, still holding his head between her hands, her eyes boring into his.

"User name. Password," she said.

He gave them to her, and she smiled, turning and tapping them into the computer.

"Very nice," she said.

Her back was to him and his eyes moved down the smooth

flesh of her body to her lovely buttocks, and the long legs beneath them. He felt his erection quiver with the desire for her, and cursed himself, trying to pull his thoughts away from sex.

"I-if you let me go I'll pay you... well... a good deal of money," he said.

She turned and smiled, then slapped his face again.

"You forgot to say mistress," she chided, turning back to the computer.

The side of his face felt hot, and he moaned weakly at the backwash of pain.

"What is your secretary's name?"

He blinked several times, panting for breath. "M-Mrs. Kensington," he gasped.

'We're just going to send her a little note telling her we'll be away for a couple of days," she said.

"Days?" he gasped.

She turned and smiled. "Perhaps less. That depends on how co-operative you are."

She turned back to him and moved behind him, then unfastened the chains holding his ankles up and apart. They fell to within an inch of the floor, and a moment later he felt his body jerk as the chain above lowered him. He groaned in relief as he was finally able to take his weight on his feet, and the pressure eased from his agonised wrists and arms.

"You see, Jeffrey? A reward for being obedient," she said.

She moved before him and pressed her bare breasts against his chest, then kissed his cheek.

"Do you want me to fuck you, Jeffrey?" she asked sweetly.

"I-I...yes, please," he whispered.

She smiled and shook her head. "You forgot to say mistress again," she reminded him.

She eased back slightly and her knee slammed up into his groin, almost lifting him off his feet. He cried out, his voice a shocked gurgle of pain, then again as her knee hammered into his groin a second time, then a third. She smiled apologetically as she did it, then stepped back as he choked and coughed, hanging by his wrists, his legs too weak and rubbery to hold him up.

"You don't learn very fast, Jeffrey," she said, tapping at the computer again.

It was several minutes before he could fight through the nausea and pain enough to talk and steady his breathing. She ignored him during this time, focused on the computer. Finally she turned to him once again, still smiling.

"Who am I, Jeffrey?"

"M-Mistress!" he gasped.

"Good boy."

She looked down at his cock and saw he had lost his erection.

"Lost a bit of our eagerness, have we? Don't worry. I'm sure it will return. Tell me the directory under which you're storing information about digital splicing, and the software your company is putting together to work with it."

He hesitated her smile turned dangerous He quickly told her where to find it.

"Good boy," she said.

"He's being obedient, is he?"

He gasped at the words, turning to see the black woman again. She was dressed in leather shorts and halter, and squeezed his bottom as she arrived.

"Yes. He wanted me to fuck him, but then he got rude."

"Silly boy. Would you like me to fuck him?"

"By all means."

Jeffrey gulped nervously, shamed anew by the black woman's presence, now feeling even more vulnerable and embarrassed, exposed to two women.

The black woman disappeared briefly, then reappeared,

still clad in the leather shorts. Now, however, she had a strange harness around her hips. His eyes widened as he saw that the harness held a thick tube shaped like an erect penis. Black, of course.

"I'm going to fuck you, Jeffrey," the woman taunted.

He gaped at her, open-mouthed.

"And you're going to like it."

She moved behind him, and he felt her fingers at his anus.

"No! Please don't!"

"You forgot to say mistress," the blonde woman said, not turning from the computer screen.

"Bad boy!' the black woman said, slapping his behind.

She was pumping her finger in and out of his anus now. She eased it out completely, and then added a second finger, laughing as he squirmed, his legs twisting, shifting his weight from one foot to the other.

'Don't worry, little boy, you'll like this," she purred.

She pulled her fingers free and he felt something larger and harder push against him. He gasped and moaned, trying to twist away, but her big hands came around him, first stroking his chest, then sliding down his belly, then gripping his thighs and yanking his legs apart. He cried out as she thrust forward, and his sphincter was forced wide by the intruding dildo.

She rolled her hips slightly, and then thrust forward again. He cried out as he felt the hard, thick dildo forced deeper into his body, then still deeper. He felt a burning and a deep ache to go along with the ache in his soul at being subjected to such indignities.

"You're going to be my little slut, baby?" she purred, grinding her hips to twist the dildo in a circular motion. "Are you going to bend over for me whenever I want it?"

She drove herself hard against him and he screamed as the dildo rammed up deep into his body, his back arching as his insides twisted and burned. She merely chuckled, her arms pinning his legs open and back, her groin now crushed against his quivering buttocks. She left it there, her hands easing off his thighs, massaging his groin and chest and belly as she kissed the nape of his neck.

"That wasn't so bad, was it, baby? You'll like this soon, don't worry."

Jeffrey moaned, ashamed. He felt his bottom jerk as the woman rolled her hips again, felt the stiff rubber penis moving within his abdomen, twisting about in the depths of his rectum. He groaned as cramps assailed him, and then groaned again, this time with relief, as she eased the thing back several inches.

"That feel better, Jeffrey?" she purred.

He did not answer, and she thrust forward again.

"Ahh. Yes! Please! Not so hard! Not... not so deep!" he begged.

"You forgot to say mistress," the blonde woman said, not looking up.

"That's right," the black woman sighed.

She gripped his hair and yanked his head back, then reached around him and slapped his flaccid cock with her hand. He screamed in shock and pain, jerking against her, trying to twist away. "You better learn some manners, Jeffrey boy," she said.

"I-I'm sorry, M-mistress," he groaned.

She began to slowly pump the dildo inside him, not plunging deep. Her hands began to caress his body again, his chest, his belly, his abdomen, then his cock, as she gently kissed and tongued his shoulder and the nape of his neck. Against his will, Jeffrey felt himself stirring. The steady stroking of the dildo in his rectum was sending very odd sensations through his body, yet they were undeniably of the pleasurable sort.

The woman removed her halter, and then pressed her warm body against his back as she continued to massage him, and he whimpered, as his cock grew thicker in her hands. She began to push the dildo deeper, and despite himself he felt the pleasure intensify. He had never felt anything like it, and caught himself before he could push himself back against her.

"Spread your legs more," she ordered.

"Y-yes, M-mistress," he breathed.

She continued her steady stroking, now pumping his cock with one hand, in time to the thrusts of the dildo inside him. His blood heated and began to race as the dildo pushed deeper still, on the edge of pain now, on the edge of cramping. Yet it felt good, and he did not understand how or why.

"You've been spending too much time with your computers, baby," she whispered. "You need to spend more time with real ladies like us."

He grunted as she thrust the dildo especially deep, a cramp rippling through his belly. Yet it faded as she pulled back, and he could feel a distinct sense of sensual pleasure as he felt the hard thickness of it sliding down, down, down the length of his rectum, until only the tip remained. He eagerly waited its return, and groaned helplessly as she slid it back in, feeling delight as it pushed through the soft folds of his flesh, jamming higher and higher until it filled him to overflowing, until his rectum and indeed, his entire abdomen, felt bloated out.

She ground herself against him, now using both hands to pump his cock, and he knew he was going to explode soon, knew he could not stop himself, and wondered why he no longer even cared to try.

He turned to see the blonde woman smirking contemptuously at him, and felt another wash of shame, yet the black woman thrust harder, and his head fell back against her shoulder as he entered his orgasm. Her fingers stroked rapidly along his cock, squeezing his balls repeatedly even as his body began to buck and jerk to her thrusting and the onset of his climax.

"My little bitch," she whispered in his ear.

CHAPTER SIX

The interview was perfunctory. They knew his education, knew his capabilities, and wanted only to ensure he was not an anti-social jerk who would disrupt the office. At its end they shook hands and Peter was led down to the Human Resources office to begin the paperwork for his hiring. That took quite some time. At its end he was shown to the office where the team was working to increase the capabilities of a processing system and introduced around.

He felt nervous the entire time, as if somehow they would suspect he was a spy, a thief, a man sent here to steal their secrets away and sabotage their programs. Worse, he thought they must somehow come to guess, no matter how impossible that might be, what lay beneath his dress trousers.

He wore no shorts. Instead he had a leather belt which buckled about his waist. A strong, soft leather strap descended from its rear, slid down between his buttocks, and up over his groin, where it widened into a round leather sac to enclose his genitals. Above this the strap narrowed again and joined the front of the belt about his waist, joined quite tightly, so tightly the centre of the belt was pulled downwards several inches.

The sac was tight against him, making him feel itchy and a little sore as it squeezed his testicles and crushed his penis. Behind him, the strap pushed out slightly just above his anus, for before sending him on his way Kathleen had forced him to bend over and forced a long, thick dildo deep into his rectum. It had hurt, at first, and then begun to feel good. Now it merely felt - odd, and oddly exciting, as well. He had to be careful how he sat, especially how quickly he sat, and were it not for the leather sac he was sure his erection would have become evident several times as his body found pleasure in the thickness and eroticism of the penetration.

The device was locked around his hips and required a small key at the centre of the belt to free the strap, so Kathleen had wryly told him to keep his drinking to a minimum, for he could not remove it himself for any reason.

He spent the rest of the day learning the processes and procedures, and studying the files for the program he was to work on. At the end of the day he drove back to SpecterWare to report to Kathleen. She had him strip first, except for the leather sac, and kneel before her as she sat at her desk, and then interrogated him on every aspect of his workday.

And when she was satisfied she turned the conversation to other aspects of his day.

"And did you enjoy the feeling of a big dildo up your backside, Peter?"

"Yes, Mistress," he said, blushing.

"And how does your cock feel?"

"Itchy and cramped, Mistress."

"And your bladder?"

"Full, Mistress," he said, face going even more red.

"You've been watching what you've been drinking?"

"Yes, Mistress. I had no coffee, just a few sips of water and a bit of juice at lunch."

"You must be thirsty then."

Kathleen poured a large glass of iced water from a jug on her desk and handed it to him. "Drink up."

He hesitated, then put the glass to his lips, feeling his bladder complain as the cold water tumbled down his throat.

"Keep drinking," she ordered.

He finished the glass, squeezing his thighs together slightly as he handed the glass back.

"Thank you, Mistress," he said.

She smiled and motioned him towards her, then turned him and opened one of the drawers of her desk. He felt a little thrill as she handcuffed his wrists together behind his back before turning him again.

She spread her legs and eased her short skirt up.

"Come, Peter, let's resume your lessons in cunnilingus."

"Yes, Mistress," he whispered.

His bladder was aching, but he fought it and bent forward, licking along Kathleen's thighs, circling her small, neat slit, and feeling a hot flush of excitement at so subservient and demeaning a position.

He pushed his face closer and closer to Kathleen's pussy, and then hesitantly let his tongue slide upwards along the neat, tight slit. Kathleen pulled on his head and he felt his face driven in hard against her pussy, felt the moisture rubbing over his skin as Kathleen ground her hips forward.

She eased up and Peter gasped, breathing again, then pushed his tongue out, sliding it between the now moist pubic lips, stroking it upwards along the cleft between them to feel for the small bump of her clitoris.

"Nasty little boy," Kathleen whispered.

She began to roll her hips slowly, grinding her sex into Peter's face as his tongue worked eagerly.

Kathleen reached down, spreading her lips, exposing her pussy hole.

"In there," she whispered. "Push your tongue in there, little slut."

Peter groaned at the word, and obeyed, his mind filled with sex-heat yet again, and marvelling at how continuous his arousal was with this woman, at the pleasure and excitement he had never felt before.

Kathleen's hand gripped his hair and tugged it lightly but painfully as she growled down at him.

"Lick! Lick," she ordered insistently. "Nasty little bastard! Lick your mistress or I shall spank your bare bottom again!"

Peter licked harder, his tongue squirming up into the blonde woman's pussy hole, lapping at her juices, then rising higher to stroke her clitoris. He was shaking with excitement at what he was doing, at the wickedness and lewdness and daring. His insides were afire with lust and he thought, weakly, that there was almost nothing he wouldn't do at that moment.

He felt the dildo within him, pressing hard against his organs, and felt the throbbing in his penis as it sought to engorge and was hindered by the tight, leather sac. There was a pain in his abdomen as well; his bladder demanding attention, but such was his excitement he found little difficulty ignoring it.

Kathleen began grinding harder and faster, her voice becoming harsher. Soft groans escaped her. Peter felt a wave of delight that he was producing such pleasure, that he was making the powerful, beautiful woman hot and excited. He licked harder, his small pink tongue lapping energetically across Kathleen's clitoris as the woman tugged on his hair and groaned in heat.

Then she arched her back with a cry that was half pleasure, half conquest, jamming Peter's face into her once again and rubbing furiously against him.

She held herself still for long moments, catching her breath, then slowly brought her head forward and down. She looked at Peter kneeling there and gripped his hair once more, then pushed him back on his heels.

"You're getting better at that, my little slut," she said.

"Thank you, Mistress," Peter said breathlessly.

"Have another glass of water."

She poured the water for him, and then held the glass to his lips. Peter knew he could not refuse, and swallowed as she tilted the glass. Some of it spilled down his chest, and he gasped at its chill, but most of it went down his throat, and he felt his bladder begin to ache fiercely.

"Be still."

"I'm sorry, Mistress," he said, clenching his teeth against the pain now throbbing in his belly.

She extended her leg, and pressed her sharp-toed shoe into his groin, grinding it against his genitals, then raised it, prodding at his abdomen. He ached and the added pressure only made it worse.

"Perhaps you'd like more water?"

"I...Mistress might I be permitted to visit the lavatory, please?" he begged.

"You sound so posh when you speak like that," she said, amused.

She poured another glass of water, and held it out to him, and he reluctantly bent forward to drink. This time she made sure to spill more over his chest, letting it trickle down his belly and along his thighs.

His ache grew. It was fierce now, almost doubling him over. He had his thighs pressed as tightly together as he could, and fought to keep from squirming under her gaze. He watched her slump lower in her chair again and raise her skirt.

"Let's try again, little slut," she ordered.

He moaned and then gasped in pain as he leaned forward. His tongue began to lick at her pussy again as her fingers combed through his hair.

"You'll make such a sweet little slave when you're trained," she said.

She raised her heels and put them on his shoulders, slumping well down in her chair now as she guided him into her sex. Soon she was rolling her hips against him once more, cursing him softly and pulling at his hair. He licked her to another orgasm, this one seemingly more powerful than the first, and felt a small wisp of satisfaction as he continued to fight the pain in his abdomen.

She sighed, looking very relaxed as she sat back in her chair.

"You've been such a good little dog, Peter," she said, "Perhaps I could do something for you now."

He prayed she would allow him to go to toilet, and his hopes sank as she instead lifted the water jug.

"Empty," she stated unhappily looking into the empty container.

She gazed at him for a moment, and then smiled. "I know. I'll give you a gift, a lovely little silver chain."

She drew one out of her desk, and then bent forward over him. He saw the chain had small clips at either end, and for a moment, wondered what she intended. Then she opened one of the clips, and pinched his nipple. He gasped, then hissed as she let the clip down around it, and it bit in tightly. A moment later the other clip bit just as tightly into his other nipple, and the silver chain hung there, its weight an insistent pull on his aching nipples.

"Now that looks lovely," she said, pleased.

"Th-thank you, Mistress," he gulped.

"Stand up, little slut."

Peter stood awkwardly, hissing slightly at the renewed pressure from his bladder. She produced a small key and unclipped the strap bound to the front of his belt, and then let the strap and sac fall away. His cock sprang out instantly erect. She turned him around and undid the belt itself, then tugged the strap out from between his clenched buttocks. The tip of the dildo was visible, and she ordered him to bend as she eased it out of his rectum.

"I think you've graduated to bigger and better things, Peter," she said.

With that she showed him another dildo, this one much thicker and longer. She pushed him against the wall and as she pulled the first out, she kicked his legs apart and shoved the second against him. He groaned in pleasure and pain as he felt the rounded head of the new dildo forcing his sphincter wider and wider. His teeth ground together and he fought to ease his muscles as Kathleen insistently jabbed and twisted the thick, studded dildo upward into his rectum.

It hurt, but the pain was minor compared to the excitement.

"That last one was a measly six inches. This one is eight. But I'm sure a big boy like you can handle it.

She pumped the dildo slowly. It was halfway inside him now, and his pain was easing. She thrust it harder and deeper, and he groaned at the pressure inside him.

She stopped, and then pulled on his nipple chain, leading him to the closet. She opened the door, and reached inside, removing a thick leather cock ring. She placed it around his shaft and below his testicles, then yanked it painfully tight and belted it in place. There was a small hook set into its bottom, and she took a weight from a shelf and hung it from the ring with an inch long chain.

Peter felt the pressure pulling down against his testicles and moaned softly, yet his excitement only grew higher.

"I have a meeting in a few minutes, Peter. It's in the boardroom, and should be quite brief. Afterwards, I may bring a friend across for a little drink here. I'm sure you know it would be unwise of you to make any noise. It would be quite embarrassing for you to be found here."

He saw that there was a hook set into the sidewall of the closet, and let out a low cry as she pulled on the chain, and swung him inside. She then raised the centre of the chain higher; forcing him onto his toes, stretching his nipples out painfully and then slipped the chain over the hook. He was able to ease back somewhat then, but still had to stay on the balls of his feet. He cried out as she placed the palm of her hand against the base of the dildo and shoved up hard, and he felt a blow, like a punch deep inside him, as she forced the dildo deeper.

"One more thing, Peter, if you make a mess in my closet I will thrash you to within an inch of your life," she said in chilly voice, her eyes glaring warningly.

Then she slid the door closed, leaving him alone.

He gazed at the wall, somewhat dazed, wondering vaguely how he had ever allowed his life to come to this.

Then again, he thought, his life had been awfully boring prior to Kathleen, and the thought of returning to that dull drudgery was not pleasant. He shifted his weight back and forth from one foot to the other, feeling increased pressure on his bladder now that he was standing, and having to remain relatively motionless. He prayed Kathleen's meeting would be quite short and that she would soon release him.

He squeezed his anal muscles down against the dildo, wondering if he felt it sliding downwards. It felt tight, his sphincter strained and stretched. His erection, along with the tight ring around the base of his cock, helped him to fight off the need to urinate, but the pressure in his lower belly was still intense.

He shifted slightly and felt the pull on his erection as the weight hanging from the cock ring swung and from side to side. He winced slightly and felt a small wave of nausea at the pressure on his testicles, then winced anew as his effort to ease that pressure pulled his nipples against the clip hooked to the wall.

He imagined he felt the dildo sliding once again, and clamped his sphincter down, then, checking to make sure it was in place, he balanced himself on one foot and drew his right heel up and back, pressing it against the base of the dildo. It was still lodged firmly in place, and he lowered his foot, gasping as the weight swung again, tugging anew on his cock.

Time passed with agonising slowness as he coped with pain and discomfort first from one source, then the other, all the time aware that he was lewdly naked in a public building where hundreds of people worked. He hoped Kathleen had at least locked her office door.

The mere thought of someone, perhaps some secretary type opening the closet door and seeing him as he was, seeing the dildo protruding from his anus, made his face flush and sent a chill of fear through him. He imagined her screaming and running out of the room, imagined people rushing in to see what the problem was, imagined them howling with laughter at him, all gathered around the closet, pointing at him in glee.

It was as if in answer to just that fear that he heard a male voice inside the office, and his heart almost stopped. It was a male voice! No, two! Then he heard a female voice, and soon Kathleen's voice intruded. He saw movements through the louvred door, and stared, bug-eyed and terrified that the door was about to be opened.

Instead he heard Kathleen talking about a new target date for release of a new product, and a marketing scheme behind the release. Several other people offered their opinions, and he heard the occasional laugh or joke as papers ruffled and chairs were pulled out or shoved in. Kathleen had a table at one end of her office not far from the closet in fact, and it seemed she had invited some of the other participants in the meeting back to her office to discuss things further.

The closet door opened, and he gaped in horror, then relaxed slightly as Kathleen smirked at him. She reached past him and drew a binder down off a shelf, then gripped the base of the dildo and pulled it out before thrusting it back in again - hard.

She withdrew, but left the door slightly ajar, thus increasing his fear and anxiety. He recognised Sally Parkins, that cute young redhead from Marketing, and Michael Sutherland, the computer engineer from Testing who seemed to smirk every time he looked at anyone he considered less skilled than himself. Every minute lasted hours, and he was completely gripped by the fear of discovery.

His erection soon disappeared, and shortly after that the pressure from his bladder began to mount. He had to clamp down harder and harder to hold himself in check, and his attention was far too focused on what was going on outside the closet to concentrate properly. He thought he heard someone say the word closet, and the word caught at him with a shock sufficient to distract him from his control.

Hot urine spurted down his leg, and when he tried to stop he found the pain simply too great. His bladder was released, and urine splashed against the wall and all down his legs. The sound of it was like a fire-hose to him in the small closet, and he imagined that at any minute one of the people in the room would open the door and see him.

He heard movement in the outer room, an increase in conversation, and felt a wave of shuddering relief as he realised they were leaving. Then the door was yanked ajar and Kathleen looked in at him. She wrinkled her nose, and then glowered angrily.

"Have you made another mess, you dirty little boy?" she demanded.

Mortified, he looked down at his feet.

"You'll have to be punished for this, little slut."

"Yes, mistress," he whispered.

***

Jeffrey reached down for his cock, and then pulled his hand away guiltily. He could not know who might be watching, when one of those women would come down and see him. What if they saw him physically abusing himself? Could he take the additional humiliation? They would snicker and laugh and tell him what a weak, pitiful fool he was.

And perhaps they would be right. He had never felt like such a low, pathetic wretch. Not only had they used him with pitiful ease, used him sexually in the most disgusting of ways, but also he had given them all the information they had asked for, putting up hardly any fight. He was too frightened of the pain they would give him, too flustered, too confused by the situation.

And now he stood naked with his hands unbound, unable to do anything to free himself. He stood impaled upon a thick pole of some sort, with a rubberised head lodged deep within his rectum. It ached, but he could not hide from himself the pleasure it gave him as well. Being naked around these beautiful women, while humiliating, seemed to have him in a near constant state of arousal. He had never imagined his body could so easily betray him against such filthy, miserable, disgusting people.

He hated them! And yet, he was fascinated, beguiled by the lewd sexual actions they forced him to participate in. His only previous sexual experiences had been masturbation, and fantasising about all the beautiful women who would never have anything to do with him. Now he was the sexual plaything of two gorgeous women. And despite the contempt with which they treated him and the anger they raised in him he was finding things not entirely unpleasant.

He could not see if he was alone. The blonde had placed a leather hood over his head, and it was locked tightly in place.

It had no holes for his eyes or nose, only one over his mouth. He had tried to pry it loose and failed. And so he was blinded, standing up, untied, but unable to do anything about his situation. He could not lift himself off the spike lodged deep inside him, and he could not move away unless he did.

And his small movements were giving him an erection as his insides shifted around the rubberised penis thing they had impaled him on.

God it was deep!

He had felt each small round ridge on the thing as it had slid into his rectum, and the blonde had told him each was half an inch apart. Fourteen of them had gone into him. Fourteen! He ran a hand along his abdomen, wondering how deep inside him the tip of the thing was, how high inside his body. It felt like it had lodged within his very bowel!

But grinding his body very slowly gave him an intensely erotic sensation, and when he raised himself onto his toes he was able to slide a good five or six inches out. That felt lovely, but not as good as when he sank back and felt it pushing back into him.

He listened for a long minute, then, hearing nothing reached for his stiff cock, gripping it and stroking it as he felt the pleasure mount. He raised himself up on his toes, and then sank back. Did it again, and again, feeling filthy and dirty as he did it, like a pervert, a sick, disgusting, weak-minded pervert. But he couldn't stop himself. The pleasure grew more powerful and he moaned inside the hood as he caressed his cock.

Crack!

He cried out at the flickering bites of pain which exploded across his buttocks, his body jerking violently, throwing his insides against the immovable post inside him, and making him grunt as if he had been punched.

"Dirty little boy!" he heard the black woman's voice say

in a scathing tone of contempt.

His face burned, but his hand reached behind him, wincing as he searched for some sign of the damage, which had been done him. That had hurt!

"You're not allowed to masturbate without my permission, you slug!"

He was too ashamed to speak.

Then something hit his chest, hard. It felt like small, thin strips. There was little weight behind them, but there were a lot of them, and they stung.

"Apologise for masturbating without permission," she ordered.

"I-I'm sorry, mistress," he said, voice shaking.

He felt the flickering blows again, this time against his groin, and cried out in fear, alarm and pain as they stung him across his thighs, belly and cock. His hands quickly covered himself, and then the things spattered against his back.

He cried out again, and reached out as if he could ward off the blows.

"Put your hands up behind your head," she ordered.

He trembled, not wanting to obey. The strips bit into his chest again, then his back, then his buttocks.

"You heard me," she said. "Or would you like me to use a heavier flog?"

"P-please I-I'm sorry, Mistress!"

"Then obey your mistress, slut. Put your hands behind your head."

His hands shook, but he slowly brought them up behind his head, his testicles trying to shrink and climb up inside him as they awaited another blow.

He was wearing restraints around his wrists, but they had not been fastened together. They were now, and worse, were clipped to the back of the collar around his neck.

"Now, boy. Tell me what you were doing," she demanded.

"I-I... nothing, mistress," he whimpered.

He cried out as the flog slashed across his groin, and the strips of soft leather rained stinging blows across his cock and testicles, across his thighs and abdomen.

"Tell me what you were doing, slut."

"I was... I was... masturbating," he whined.

He wished he could sink into the floor.

"Did I tell you could masturbate?" she asked in a reasonable tone.

"No, mistress," he said miserably.

"If I want you to feel pleasure I will give it to you. Do you understand, slut?"

"Yes, mistress."

"Because you have tried to give yourself pleasure without asking permission you will have to be punished. Do you understand, slut?"

"Y-Y-Yes, mistress," he whispered.

"Try to take it like a man, you slug."

The flog lashed his back and he jerked and quivered. It landed again, and again, and again, slow, measured blows which stung and burned. Yet he held still and did not cry out. Then the blows landed against his chest, and he clamped his jaw closed, fighting the pain. The flog moved lower, the sparkles of stinging, snapping pain erupting across his upper stomach, then his abdomen, and then they began to strike his crotch and thighs. His cock ached and he cried out several times, tears filling his eyes. He jerked against the post, and it shifted inside him.

After a dozen blows, however, he realised the pain did not seem to be growing worse. His crotch throbbed hotly, burned with pain, yet the severity was tolerable, and the continuous nature of the pain served to block the shock of the sudden stings from the new blows.

He became aware that his cock, which had gone soft, was

growing hard again, and this was making the stings worse. He was confounded by this, and by the sense of sexual need he felt inside him. Yet he was in no position to do anything about it.

The blows stopped and the woman moved closer to him, her arm brushing his chest. A moment later he felt the post within him begin to sink away. He felt some relief, both from the pressure inside him and the thought that his beating was over. His skin felt sore and hot, as though he had mild sunburn, all down his back, buttocks, chest and groin.

The post slipped out of him and he sagged on his feet until she jerked him forward. She released his restraints, letting his hands to fall to his sides.

"Down on your hands and knees, slut!"

He obeyed, frightened by the strength and tone of her voice, wondering if he would be further punished.

He felt her lift his right ankle up and press it back against his buttock, then strap it there against his upper thigh. A moment later she did the same to his left ankle. Something was pushed into his still partially open anus, something round, which his anus closed behind.

"Now crawl, dog."

He felt a pull of the collar, and crawled forward in that direction. His knees ached on the cold stone, and he could feel grit and dirt against the palms of his hands. Something soft and loose, like hair, was brushing against the backs of his thighs. After a few moments he realised it was some sort of tail, which must be attached to the round thing she had pushed into his bottom. His mind blanked momentarily in utter wonder, and then his hands struck something wooden.

"There are stairs here. Climb them," he was ordered.

This was awkward, but not difficult. He took them one at a time and then felt tile beneath his hands. Something snapped at his buttocks and he yelped and lurched forward.

"Faster, slut," she ordered.

He crawled faster, letting the pull of the leash guide him.

A leash, he thought wonderingly. I'm on a bloody leash, naked, with a tail thing hanging down behind me like a dog, like a beast!

"Would you like something to drink, slut?"

"Yes, mistress!" he exclaimed.

His throat was parched and his mouth had been feeling uncomfortably dry for some hours, yet he had known better than to ask for anything.

He felt her hand against him, moist, and drew back slightly, confused.

"Come on, slut. Drink," she ordered.

And he understood, with another little shock of wonder that he was to drink out of her hand. They were turning him into a beast.

Yet he was too thirsty to let what shreds of pride he retained stop him. He put his mouth forward and slurped the small bit of water out of her hand. She pulled it away, then brought it back again, and he repeated his actions as she patted his head through the hood.

"Good little dog," she cooed. "Good little slut."

She let him have more water like that, then set down a bowl and let him drink out of it. He had to drink as a dog would, and was not permitted to use his hands, but he didn't really care at that point. The water was cool and delicious, and he drank thirstily until the bowl was empty.

"Are you hungry, dog?"

"Yes, mistress," he said, feeling pleasure and misery simultaneously, knowing he would have to eat out of her hand.

And indeed, that was the case. He was forced to lick pieces of sausage from her fingers and take them out of the palm of her hand, all the while being petted and stroked.

"Now let's see what else you're hungry for," she said.

CHAPTER SEVEN

Jeffrey felt her hand stroking backwards to his bottom, then massaging his testicles and caressing his cock. It took little effort to bring him erect again, and she moved away, then he heard her in front of him, at his own level now.

"Mount me, dog," she called from in front of him. "Do it like the animal you are."

He felt something pushing back against his face, and his lips tasted the softness of flesh. He reached up and felt her hips before him, then, his excitement rising, he rose as best he could, pulling himself over her, feeling his way up her body. He marvelled at how slim and soft she felt, how fresh and clean her scent was.

"Now, slut. Service your mistress," he heard.

Madness, he thought wonderingly. This is all madness!

Yet he felt for her sex, slipped his fingers against it then pierced her and drove himself into her body. He heard her groan softly, and knew at least a small sense of pride, of male domination as he mounted her and began thrusting.

"Harder, you pitiful wimp. Ride me like a demon!"

The voice seemed to come from far away, but he had had no food in some time, and was quite disoriented by the treatment they had given him these past two days.

He began thrusting into her furiously, his hands clasped around her body, fingers squeezing her breasts. He laid his belly and chest down atop hers, knowing an animalistic pleasure as his cock stroked powerfully inside the woman's sex. He felt her begin to buck beneath him, to thrust her haunches back at him, and this increased the force of his thrusts. Yet her voice showed no pain, only excitement as she called upon him to take her faster still.

It was like riding a wild, bucking horse, and yet he clung to her with a thrill of excitement he had rarely felt, trying to hold her in place with his hands. Trying to feel for the direction of her movements, to stay mounted as she threw her hips back against him and growled like a beast herself.

'Do it! Do it! Do it! Bastard! Filthy slut! Is that all you have! Give me more!"

His hips and belly ached, but he did his best to ride her harder still, his entire body jarred by the impact each time it met her backside, each time his cock rammed home in her tight depths.

Her upper body began to twist and jerk from side to side, and he clung to her desperately, still driving himself furiously into her pussy as he heard her grunt and pant in pleasure. He wondered if she was coming, and then knew a frantic worry over whether she would throw him off or let him finish himself.

She was making a low panting sound, but he hardly heard it above his own pounding heart and the roaring in his head. He felt himself on the edge of exploding, and knew he had only seconds before he filled her belly with his seed.

And then he was thrown off to land heavily on his back on the floor, dazed and still instinctively thrusting his hips.

"Enough, dog. It's time to take you walkies."

He felt a sharp pull on his collar, and weakly rolled onto his front again, getting to hands and knees.

"Come, dog."

He crawled after her, and then over a low trestle. He felt cool air on his body, and heard the sound of birds. Then his fingers came down on grass and his head turned from side to side as if he could see where he might be and tell whether anyone was nearby that he might call to for assistance.

Assistance! He couldn't possibly do so! What if he were rescued like this? The humiliation of that was more than he could possibly bear.

"What's the matter, doggie?" she purred. "Does your little

pee-pee need to be milked?"

He felt her hands beneath his legs, squeezing his still-erect cock, and gasped, instinctively thrusting into her hand. She began to stroke her fingers rapidly up and down and he moaned helplessly. New shame filled him, and a terrible fear that someone might see him here outdoors. Yet he could not resist her rough masturbatory movement, and soon his semen was spewing out onto the grass beneath as his hips rutted downwards into her pumping fist.

"Good dog," she said, patting his rump.

"Now, dog," Yvette said, "we were about to see to training you, weren't we?"

Jeffrey had no idea. "Yes mistress," he said automatically.

"Now, Jeffrey. We're going to learn some tricks. Won't that be nice?"

"Yes, mistress," he said again automatically.

"Good. First, I want you to sit up and beg. That's done, as you would expect, just like a dog would, back straight. Good. Put your arms out and your paws down, straight down. Good dog. Now let your tongue hang out. That's a good dog."

She petted his head, and then moved around him.

"Now lie down on the floor. Good. Roll over onto your back."

Jeffrey obeyed, grunting at the awkwardness of moving with his ankles tied back to his thighs.

"Spread your legs wider apart. We don't want to hide your little pee-pee do we?"

"No, Mistress."

"Now get back on your knees. Good, raise your bottom high and let your shoulders and face down against the floor. Spread your legs more. Excellent. Wag your tail for us, slut."

Jeffrey dutifully wiggled his behind from side to side so that the tail brushed against his thighs.

Although he could not see he held a mental image in his mind of what he was doing, of the sight he must present to the big black woman. It would have been a humiliating sight, except, of course, that it was difficult to be humiliated any further. It was still somewhat shaming, but the shame was a low thing, gnawing at his belly. Over it was a strange sense of sexual fascination. He had been missing so much in his dull life of computer programming and engineering. He should have found a woman long since, a woman with a soft body and hard attitude who would teach him the pleasures to be had in life, away from a keyboard.

He felt a blow of pain across his bottom, and moaned, but held his position.

"Dirty little boy," she taunted.

He heard her moving around in front of him, feet scuffing on the floor.

"My boots got quite dirty while taking you for walkies, Jeffrey," she said. "I think you should do something about that."

"Yes, mistress," he replied.

He hesitated.

"What mistress?"

"Clean them, idiot!"

A blow to the side of the head set his ears ringing.

"Yes, mistress," he grunted.

He reached out, only to have his hands batted away.

"With your tongue, Jeffrey."

He felt a little quiver of excitement mixed with the outrage this order brought. Yet the mental image of himself licking the woman's boots was strangely irresistible, and he bent down low, searching for her boot, then finding it and licking at it with his tongue. He licked down the top, then around the sides, moved back to the toe, then, as he felt her foot rise, made a moaning sound and angled his head down so as to lick the underside.

Then, of course, he repeated this action on the other boot.

All the while she rained abuse on him, telling him what a vile, filthy, disgusting, pitiful little man he was, and Jeffrey was gripped by alternating bouts of shame and excitement.

Finally she had him crawl down a narrow hall, before removing his leash.

"You can stay in this room for a while. There's a bowl of water on the floor if you can find it."

He heard her chuckle, and then the door closed. He crawled awkwardly along on elbows and knees, face low to the floor, not wanting to overturn the bowl by mistake, for he was still quite thirsty. It was quite a small room, as it turned out, perhaps six or seven feet on a side, and he had little difficulty finding the bowl in a corner. He paused, wondering if he was permitted to drink. Then, his thirst getting the better of him, he lowered his mouth and did so.

***

SpecterWare stock rose thirty-four percent on rumours of some major development concerning the company's products. In the furious world of technology stocks this was not very much remarked upon, but shareholders were quite gratified, as was the board of directors. They demanded to know, however, what it was Kathleen was working on that may have provoked such an advance. She hinted at the information she had recently obtained from Jeffrey Fitzwilliams but said the project was still in the early stages of development.

Also in the early stages of development was Peter Cross' training. Kathleen thought she had him fairly well under control now, and the degree to which he would allow himself to be humiliated was gratifying, but she liked her little toys to be as fully committed to her as possible, and Peter obviously needed further discipline.

To that end, and to give her time to work on some other

problems, she had placed him in the basement atop a long, narrow wooden table. The table was ancient, the wood scarred and cracked. It was quite low, not much higher than a chair, really, and not much wider than Peter's own body. She'd found it at an antique sale, and had no idea what its original purpose had been. She had fitted restraints to one end - which was a simple enough task, and attached a modern block and tackle to other.

That was considerably more complicated a task, and she and Yvette had worked and cursed at it for quite some days before it had begun to work properly.

Peter lay upon it now, stretched out nicely, the fine muscles of his body quite visible as he lay beneath her gaze. His wrists were, of course, bound to the restraints above his head, which in turn, were attached to the block and tackle, and it took very little effort at all to turn the crank so that Peter's body quivered with tension.

She found it an attractive sight, and felt again that rush of pleasure, which accompanied her domination of a handsome man. She let her hands trail lazily across his body, enjoying her control over him, exulting in the fact he not only was willing to suffer pain for her but so worshipped her he was glad, even aroused by it.

"Enjoy yourself, little slut," she whispered.

With him secure and occupied, she went to her small office at home and phoned people she knew who either owed her favours or who hoped to earn favours from her. Most of the latter group was men, of course, and few of them would ever get the favour they so earnestly desired.

But they proved useful anyway. In a mere two hours she was able to substantially add to her knowledge of which technology firms were involved in which types of promising research.

She was still on the phone in the late evening when Yvette

came home.

"Have a good day at work?" Kathleen asked teasingly.

Yvette snorted and fell heavily into the chair beside her. Then she reached down into her small black purse and drew out a thick wad of notes, dumping them onto the table. They were all ten and twenty pound notes.

"I see we were a popular girl again today."

"Yeah, I swear to Christ I'm making so much money at this place I don't even need the stock market."

Kathleen smiled. "It's nothing compared to what we can get on the market."

"I made over four hundred pounds today. That club is filled with desperate little nerdy computer types who have tons of money and very little time in which to spend it."

"That's why we had you work there, Yvette," Kathleen said sarcastically.

"Yeah, yeah, I know. But it's so different. These guys are pathetic. I think I could have most of them eating out of the palm of my hand without even taking my clothes off."

"But would they pay you four hundred pounds a night to eat?"

Yvette snorted in amusement.

"I got a hot one tonight. He works for Armstrong. He says they're working on something that will make all my fears and worries about buying lingerie on the Internet go away."

"How interesting. Anything specific?"

"Something to do with broadband phase shifting. I'll run into him tomorrow like I did that Grant boy and get him to invite me home."

Kathleen nodded. All these little computer types had powerful home computers, and all of them worked on their projects there at times. And while the little man was tied up in the bedroom, Yvette could explore his computer and take what she wanted. It wouldn't give them the kind of massive and thorough project information they were getting from Jentech, but it would certainly give them enormous pointers to where that information could be found.

"So where's our boy Peter?"

"Downstairs on the rack."

"I knew you'd find a reason to put him on that," Yvette said with a smile.

"He's being properly punished." Kathleen scowled.

"Can I go down and punish him some more?"

"Be my guest. I would have thought you'd get enough of that at the strip club."

"I never get enough," Yvette said, grinning as she stood.

Kathleen watched her go, feeling only a slight resentment at the woman making use of her toy. She had met Yvette at a gym a few years earlier, and admired the woman's strength of character, as well as her powerful physique. She would never turn her own body into that mass of muscles Yvette carried around, and silently thought the woman somewhat mad to have done so. But she found it hard to relate to weak men, or weak women, and had allowed herself to be seduced by Yvette.

Their relationship was an odd one. Neither was in love with the other, although there was some affection, and both were principally occupied with men, who they considered weak and easily manipulated. It was Kathleen who had introduced Yvette to the true depths that manipulation and control could go, to the pleasure of holding sexual power over another, but Yvette had learned quickly.

Yvette knew little about technology, and had dropped out of school. She had been working as a waitress and part-time stripper when Kathleen had found her. Together they had mused aloud about the means to gather riches to themselves, but Yvette had always acquiesced to Kathleen in things which required planning and educated knowledge. And it had been

Kathleen who had decided on their current course of action.

She toyed with the idea of joining Yvette downstairs, but discarded it. She had further work to do, and Yvette deserved her little bit of sport with Peter.

***

The strain on Peter's body did not seem terribly painful at first. His wrists certainly ached from the pull, and his arms were under quite a degree of strain, but it was tolerable. At first. However, as the seconds became minutes and the minutes wore on he began to feel the ache spreading through his body, up his legs and down his arms to his spine, and through his spine to his chest and shoulders. It was unnatural to be so tightly constricted, under such pressure, and unable to move at all for any length of time, and his body began to protest. It began to cramp and ache with growing fierceness, and he had no way at all to ease his discomfort.

Yvette came down the stairs and Peter jerked his head to the left, staring anxiously and breathlessly at her. The woman slid her gloved hand along his body to his groin and slipped her fingers about his cock.

"Are you getting a nice rest, Peter?" she asked tauntingly.

"Yes mistress," he replied, his voice somewhat shaky.

"Not too tired? Too sore?"

She massaged his cock, which was soft and cold in the basement air.

"No Mistress, he gulped.

Her hand stretched out his cock as she examined it, then she walked around above the table. He tried to pull his head back far enough to see her but could not.

"You have been a bad, bad boy," she said. "Making a mess like that in Kathleen's closet. Honestly. We at least thought you were potty trained."

Peter blushed.

She came to the side of the table, and he saw that she was now nude, her body as powerful and beautiful as he remembered. Her long hair was loose and spilled down her back, hanging around her face gleaming lustrously. She stepped gracefully across the low table, straddling it, then knelt on its hard surface, her knees barely fitting on either side of his hips, pressing in tightly against his soft flesh. She slid slowly up his body as her brown eyes caught his, her soft sex and buttocks caressing him all the way up, sliding across his belly and chest until she was kneeling directly over his head.

"Let's see what you've learned, hmmm," she said.

She settled her sex down against his mouth, her thighs pressing against the sides of his head, then leaned her head down to smile at him.

Peter found himself determined to show her how very much he had already learned at the hands of her and Kathleen. And despite the growing pain in his body he set out to do so. His tongue slid up and down against her sex in long seductive motions, teasing and caressing as she settled atop him. Sensing her impatience, however, he soon pushed himself up between the soft lips of her sex. He had had a great deal more practice, and his tongue and jaw were considerably stronger than when Kathleen had first chained and used him, and soon the black woman was grinding down with obvious pleasure, her sex wet, her juices dripping into his mouth as he tongued her.

He became so intent on his work he hardly noticed his cock was becoming erect, nor paused to consider that he was a prisoner being used and tormented. All he cared about was proving to Yvette not only his abilities as a lover but also his strength as a man.

His tongue whipped upwards across the woman's clitoris, and he felt a grim satisfaction at her barely audible groan of pleasure. He circled her swollen, glistening bud with his tongue, easing away as she tried to direct herself back against him, then, sensing she was about to force him, he shot his tongue back against it, rasping furiously back and forth and drawing forth another groan of pleasure.

He felt a fierce exultation as her movements became quick and frantic, as her sex was jammed furiously against his face and ground back and forth, as she began to gasp and pant with excitement and more moisture poured through her sex. She bounced atop his face as she came, grunting in ecstasy, and then sagged against him before slowly easing back.

"Not bad," she said with a weary smile.

"Thank you Mistress," he said, a trifle arrogantly.

"But we'll see how much energy you have for the long haul."

She slipped off him and off the table, then left him alone there.

Without her presence the ache in his body returned to the forefront of his mind, growing worse with each passing minute. He was sweating now, both from the heat and the pain, and could feel the rough wood against his naked back and buttocks.

His cramps and aches grew worse, and with them an intense and terrible frustration at his complete immobility. He could not budge, nor bend, nor twist his arms or legs or back even a fraction of an inch. He began to think of how wonderful, how lovely it would be to simply bend his legs, to sit up so that his back was bent, to pull his arms in against his body.

Kathleen returned, abruptly pulling him out of the absorption with his own pain and discomfort.

"Peter," she said. "Do tell me you're enjoying your stay with us."

"Yes, I... I am Mistress," he gasped.

"You're such a weak man, Peter," she said.

She took his cock in her hands and began to lightly stroke it.

"You do have a nice body, though," she said, her other hand sliding up along his chest.

"Th-Thank you, Mistress," he gulped.

He was hardening, and he stared at her desperately, hoping she would free him to let him touch her with his hands.

The hand on his chest slipped down to join the other caressing his erection, then she closed both hands around his testicles - and squeezed.

Peter let out an explosive cry of pain and shock, and she smiled gently.

"Are you sorry for making such a mess in my office, Peter?"

He groaned in pain and nausea, and then cried out once more as she squeezed him once again, this time maintaining the pressure. His body shuddered and trembled as he strained against the bonds holding him. His insides felt on fire, and he screamed aloud at the tremendous agony.

"I'm sorry! I'm sorry, Mistress!"

She released her hold and he sobbed in relief, chest heaving.

She patted his cheek, then moved to the head of the table, and Peter felt the pressure increase on his arms, wrists, shoulders and spine. He hardly cared at first, for the pain still throbbing through his groin.

She walked to the stairs and began to climb. "Not now, perhaps," she called after her, "but soon, you'll be allowed to sleep upstairs with the humans."

The light turned off, and he was left alone with his pain.

The minutes passed, turning to hours. He groaned aloud without knowing it, his body unbearably taut and aching. He wondered if his arms and legs could actually be pulled from their sockets by the pressure of the table.

The rack. That was what it was. He had, of course, heard of them in old stories, but never had he imagined the pain such a simple device could mete out.

He groaned again, moaning and half-sobbing, hardly aware of it as he stared upwards. Sweat coated every inch of his body now, and his boyish fringe was plastered against his forehead.

"Peter? Are you enjoying your stay?"

He groaned in response and Kathleen chuckled.

"I thought you might be thirsty," she said.

She did something above him, hanging a rope, he thought. Then he saw it was a pencil thin hose she had uncoiled from somewhere. She hung it in place well above him, and then adjusted it slightly. A drop of water plummeted down onto his forehead, then another.

"There," she said, satisfied.

With that she disappeared, and Peter winced as another drop hit his forehead. He was quite thirsty, in truth, but try as he might he could not bend his head back, shift his mouth upwards, enough to let the water fall into it. Instead it fell implacably down on that spot over the table where his forehead rested. He turned his head to one side, and that helped for a time, yet the remorseless drops of water were preying on his mind more and more as time passed. He came to dread the soft impact of each individual drop, timing them, knowing exactly when each was due.

His body ached, and he moaned and cursed and then sobbed in misery, pulling furiously against the restraints holding him, then slumping helplessly, exhausted, staring up as the water continued to fall one large drop at a time.

CHAPTER EIGHT

"I can't say very much of course," Charles said, looking over his drink at the two young men. "Confidentiality agreements, you know."

The two, both young eager brokers, nodded eagerly, even impatiently.

"But, well, if I was looking to make a name for myself, I'd stop looking at the tried and true, and start looking where no one expects."

"Outside tech?" one asked in surprise.

"No, dear boy," Charles said tolerantly. "At tech companies no one else is looking at."

"But isn't there generally a reason why no one is watching them?"

"Of course. Because no one expects anything of them. And that's because most of them are dogs. But there are a few which may prove... surprising over the next few months."

"Such as?"

Charles looked away, then back again. "There's a little company right here in London, as a matter of fact, called SpecterWare."

"SpecterWare? Never heard of it."

Charles smiled knowingly.

"That, my lad, is how you make your reputation, by getting in early on a real comer."

"What makes you think this SpecterWare is a comer?"

"Well, as I said, it wouldn't be ethical for me to disclose inside information. But I would point out that if you investigated this company you'd find there had been a change of leadership recently, and that the place has undergone a real house cleaning and a readjustment of goals and expectations. Their marketing team has been completely replaced and expanded, too."

He scratched his nose idly and looked around.

"I wouldn't be at all surprised to find that SpecterWare had a slew of innovative new products in final testing. Others would be, of course. But not me."

The two young brokers looked at each other excitedly.

***

"You're looking very pretty, Peter," Kathleen said, smiling and patting his cheek.

"Th-thank you, Mistress," he said anxiously.

Peter's long night of torment had ended with him being given a washing by Yvette who also massaged his aching muscles to relieve some of the stress and tension in them. Then Kathleen had let him eat breakfast - on his knees, of course, and he'd been sent off to work as usual. He hadn't accomplished an awful lot for Jentech, but then again, that wasn't his goal. His goal was to find out all he could about the products Jentech was developing and report back to Kathleen.

Now, with early evening approaching, he still ached all over, and still felt oddly taller, but he was capable of standing up without stumbling, and hardly trembled at all. He was wearing tight leather shorts which zipped up both hips, a studded leather collar, and wrist and ankle restraints. The ankle restraints were free. The wrist restraints were clipped together behind his back. A leash was attached to the collar. It hung loosely as he sat in the passenger seat of his car, looking nervously about him at the traffic and pedestrians.

"Afraid someone will see you?"

"I... yes, mistress," he confessed.

"They will. Many people will. I want people to see what a lovely little man toy I have. They'll be so jealous of me."

Peter did not answer that, wondering again how he had let

himself get into this kind of a situation. He was aroused, as he always seemed to be around Kathleen, but quite anxious about what she planned for him, and who, besides Yvette, might see him dressed as he was.

The car passed through heavy traffic, and a woman in a car next to theirs turned idly and blinked her eyes in surprise at the bare-chested man wearing the collar. He looked away quickly, blushing. He was simply not the exhibitionistic sort, or at least, never had been before. The only place he had ever gone bare-chested was the beach, and even there he'd been slightly uneasy at first.

The car turned down a narrow side street, and he looked around at the lack of light and traffic with a measure of relief. Then he saw a more brightly lit building. It looked like an old Victorian era mansion, except someone with poor decorating skills had strung red Christmas lights along its roofline and twined them about the wooden rose pillars supporting its low porch roof.

His anxiety skyward as Kathleen pulled up before it and stopped.

"Where are we going, Mistress?" he asked again.

"Wherever I choose to go, slave."

She opened her door, then closed it and went around to the passenger side.

"I-I'd rather go home now," he said worriedly.

She smiled and took his leash, forcing him out of the car. He stared around fearfully, his bare feet cold on the pavement. To be dressed in nothing but a pair of shorts in the middle of the city was simply too bizarre for him. It wasn't proper! And to be bound out in the open! What would people think if they saw him like this?

Kathleen led him down the small path, which led to the porch, and he followed hurriedly, eager to be out of the street where people would see him, would point and snicker.

Kathleen knocked at the door, and a tall man dressed in leather opened it. He even had a leather hood.

"Come," he said, looking briefly at Peter, who flushed red under the dark-eyed gaze.

Kathleen tugged on his leash and led Peter inside.

The place had been an old Victorian mansion, and the internal layout appeared to have been preserved. They walked into a front hall and he saw doorways leading off in three directions, and a wide winding staircase leading upstairs. Yet he barely noticed them. For the place, though not crowded, had many people standing and sitting about drinking and chatting. The lights were dim, but bright enough for him to want to disappear into the floor as eyes, both male and female, turned his way.

Many of the people there were dressed scantily, and leather appeared to be a preference. He was not the only man there who was bare-chested, nor indeed the only one with a collar. Yet he cringed anyway, horrified at being publicly exposed in such a fashion. Several people smirked at him, and he turned his eyes to the floor, mortified.

"Come, slut," Kathleen said her voice loud enough for anyone nearby to hear.

His face flamed still further, and he was grateful to be led through one of the doorways. Just inside he was amazed to see a woman, utterly naked, squatting on a low platform. She was pierced by two metal probes attached to the platform, one going into her pussy, and the other into her rectum. Her nipples were pierced, and wire was tied to each ring, pulling them out painfully far. Several people were gathered around her, and before Kathleen tugged him away he saw a man pull her dark hair back painfully far and scratch at the soft flesh of her breast with a strange little claw.

Then they were pushing through crowds of people and into another room. There was a naked man here, standing almost proudly near the far wall. He was quite well built, an older man with hair on his wide, powerful chest.

His arms were raised high and encased in shackles, the shackles chained up and apart to pillars flanking him. A woman stood behind him, and as he watched she brought a long, thin whip slashing down across his back. He closed his eyes briefly, and seemed to groan, but did not otherwise react. He had an erection, and the base of it was encased in the same kind of ring which Peter was himself familiar with.

Kathleen led them around to the rear, and he could now see the man's back and buttocks were criss-crossed by angry red welts. He watched, and winced, as the whip came down again, cutting into his back between his shoulders.

"Wouldn't you like to be up there, little slut?" Kathleen whispered.

Peter stared at her in terror. Up there? Naked? With all those people watching him?

There were three or four dozen people standing about watching the show, and he wondered how it was the man did not hide his eyes in shame as they laughed and joked, making comments about his backside and his cock.

The woman lashed the long whip out again, but this time she was closer, and the tip of the whip curled around the man's hip to strike at his abdomen. He gasped aloud, and several of the audience members giggled or applauded. The woman with the whip wore a red leather bra and matching trousers along with white flats. She had her long hair tied back in a ponytail and each time she swung the whip the tail swung out wildly behind her.

She swung it again, and the whip again curled around the man's hip, this time slicing lower, and the tip cutting into the flesh of his inner thigh. He hissed and jerked, his body moving, but held in place. Kathleen led Peter around to the front, where most of the rest of the audience was now moving, and in the crowd someone groped his buttocks through his leather shorts.

He gasped and his head jerked around but he could not see who had done it.

The woman with the whip waited for her audience to reposition itself, then swung again. Once more the whip cut across the man's hip, this time on the other side, and the tip bit into his abdomen just above the base of his cock. He arched his back, crying out in pain, and catcalls greeted his weakness.

They were in the midst of the crowd now, and another hand slipped down between his legs, squeezing and groping him. He tried to see who it was but Kathleen had his leash tightly held, and he could not even turn around. Nor did he think it likely she would do anything if he complained. So he stood watching the man, face burning as a hand kneaded him through his tight leather shorts.

The whip curled around his hip again and this time snapped at his cock. He screamed, his body twisting violently, and the audience applauded.

A hand was massaging Peter's bottom now, and he tried to get Kathleen's attention.

The whip swung forward again, and once more snapped at the man's cock, sending it bouncing wildly as he roared in pain.

Fingers began to slowly unzip the zipper at his left hip, and Peter again tried to get Kathleen's attention.

The whip swung again, and again, and each time it curled around the man's left or right hip to bite at his cock. Peter was both fascinated and repulsed, amazed the man could sustain an erection through that kind of assault, through the obvious pain he was going through as he twisted and pulled frantically at the metal shackles.

He felt the zipper snap all the way down, and the side of

his shorts let go. The shorts were really two separate pieces of leather attached by zippers down either hip. With one released it fell away, leaving him naked, and his eyes bulged as he struggled to keep from making any sound or movement, which would alert the crowd to his nudity. Kathleen still held his leash tightly in her hand, the leash going over her shoulder and attached to a ring set in the middle of his collar. He could not turn his head and could not resist as a hand squeezed his cock and balls. Fingers slid around his cock and began to pump up and down.

"Kathleen," he gasped.

The noise of the crowd was too loud for his words to be heard, and he pushed his body desperately against her, only to have her head twist and her eyes glare coldly at him.

A finger pushed against his anus, then wriggled up inside him, and he paled, trying to pull free.

The whip slashed against the man's cock once again, and he came, spurting his juices out onto the floor in front of him as the audience jeered and applauded. As the crowd began to break up Kathleen turned and tugged on his leash, leading him across the room.

"Stop!" he gasped, "Stop!"

She turned to glare at him, and suddenly seemed to notice his shorts had fallen off.

"What have you done with your shorts?" she demanded crossly.

The injustice of such a question, in light of his bound hands, momentarily struck Peter dumb, and then as more people began noticing his nudity he tried to hide behind her.

"Someone unzipped them!" he gasped. "Get me something to wear!"

"Well you should have said something at the time," she replied, unconcerned. "Besides, you have a lovely bottom, and a very nice cock. You needn't be ashamed of them."

"Doesn't he have a lovely cock, Martha?" she asked a passing woman.

The woman, her hair done up in a column high above her head, wearing a brief black silk dress which barely covered her groin looked down and smiled, then reached forward and lifted his cock to hold it in her hand. She gave it a measuring squeeze, lips pursed.

"It's not too bad," she said. "Got some nice thickness. You ought to have it pierced though."

Face red, Peter stared at her, appalled. Pierced?

"See, little dog? Nothing to be ashamed of," Kathleen said.

She tugged on the leash and led him into another room. This one had fewer people, and so all could see the full extent of his nudity. Eyes glinted and lips turned up in smiles and snickers. People whispered as they watched him being led across the room.

Peter's mind spun and he thought he might actually pass out from the shock of being so exposed before all these strangers. He had never imagined he could bear such humiliation, nor that he would ever be subjected to it. Yet Kathleen led him along, utterly unconcerned, pausing to chat to people, ignoring his strangled appeals to get his shorts, or find something else to cover him with.

They passed a pair of men, and one of the men turned and gave his bottom a squeeze, smirking when Peter turned appalled eyes on him.

"This way," Kathleen ordered, pulling him through another doorway.

Each room contained new people to stare and snicker at him, new people to make Peter's shame burn deep into his belly. Hands squeezed and groped him as they passed, or on occasion Kathleen would stop to speak to someone, usually a woman, and point out the size and shape of his manhood while Peter stood helpless and still.

He was in a bit of a daze after a while, hardly able to credit that this was happening. That he could be walking naked amid a crowd of people, or standing naked while Kathleen and a pair of women looked at his cock, occasionally pinched or prodded it, and discussed its merits.

They walked up the stairs, and down a narrow hall, emerging in another large room. There were perhaps a dozen people gathered, so things were far from crowded. Kathleen led him to one side and had him stand still, and then she reached above her and pulled down a pair of chains, which hung from the roof, quickly attaching them to the rings of his ankle restraints.

"Kneel, my little slut," she ordered.

He knelt, glad to be able to hide himself a little, to close his thighs around his genitals and cover them from view.

She bent over above him, smiling.

"Did you think I was pretending when I told you that you would be severely punished for mucking up my closet?"

He stared at her in shock. "But... but, I couldn't help it!" he exclaimed in a harsh whisper, hoping no one could hear.

"That has nothing to do with anything," she said. "Now I don't want you to embarrass me by making too much noise."

He stared at her, unable to understand her meaning.

She pushed him back so he fell on his backside on the floor then nodded to a man who stood across the room by the wall. The man turned a crank and Peter felt the chains pull taut against his ankles. He stared at them in shock, wondering what was happening, and then gasped, as they pulled harder still, lifting his feet into the air. He turned to stare at Kathleen, but she turned her back to him and made her way towards the wall, where a collection of whips stood on a shelf. The other people in the room began to form a semi-circle, all facing him, and more people began to enter the room behind him.

Appalled, horrified, Peter's mouth opened and closed repeatedly, yet no words emerged. The chains pulled upwards, raising his legs still further, pulling up until he fell back onto his back, and then raising his hips off the floor. He could hear some of the comments from the crowd now, obscene comments about his body, and about the things they wanted to do to him. The chains lifted his back up, so that now only his shoulders were pressed into the floor. He whimpered helplessly as they lifted him higher still.

And then he was hanging freely from his ankles, and his legs were wide apart, exposing him completely to the view of the crowd of strangers looking on.

Someone snapped on a light, and a spotlight shone down upon him, drawing back the veil of dim light, which had slightly protected his privacy. White light exposed his pale flesh to the crowd, who giggled and made jokes as Kathleen chose the whip, which would punish him for his disobedience.

She set aside a long flog, one with three foot strips of lightweight leather, then went to another shelf and removed two powerful vibrators before returning to where he hung. The vibrators clicked on, and the crowd quieted as she began to play them across his groin.

She moved them slowly around his testicles, then along the shaft of his flaccid manhood. She caressed his anal opening, and slid one up and down between his splayed buttocks. The man moved forward with a small jar of something and she dipped the head of one of the vibrators into it, and then pressed it against his anal opening.

Peter cringed and moaned and whimpered as, before several dozen people, she slowly pushed the vibrator down into his rectum. She pumped it lightly up and down, forcing it ever deeper, twisting it lightly from side to side as she worked.

Peter felt his insides begin to ache at the depths of the penetration felt cramps rippling along his belly. But he dared not speak. His tongue was clamped to the roof of his jaw by the degree of shame and humiliation he felt.

She forced the thing deep and left it there, the tip jutting out then began to work on his cock again. She massaged his testicles and cock, using the vibrator against the head, and Peter moaned in despair as he began to stiffen. He could not see the people watching now. He could hardly make out anything, upside down as he was, with the bright light shining directly down on him. That was a blessing, yet it helped, along with the blood rushing to his brain, to confuse and daze him.

He felt the vibrator pumping slowly in and out again. His rectum had adjusted somewhat to it, but then it was removed and another inserted in its place. He could tell this was a different one because it was certainly thicker. He groaned to feel his insides forced wide, wondering how thick the thing could be. His sphincter muscle stung and ached as Kathleen jammed it deeper and deeper, and then he began to feel those cramps and aches at the pit of his belly once more, while the thing buzzed furiously inside him.

He had a full erection now, and Kathleen displayed it to the room, which responded with applause and obscene remarks.

He felt his arms released, the clips holding the restraints together undone, but almost before he realised it his arms were pulled straight down below him and the restraints clipped to a ring set in the floor.

Kathleen forced the vibrator deep, and he grunted at the pain, then she moved away. He stared about him dizzily, blinking his eyes as Kathleen came in front of him. Something dangled to the floor beside her, dragging along as she moved. It was a whitish brown thing, quite long and...

She swung her arm and the whip flew sideways, the long

strips cutting across his bare chest. He yelped in surprise and pain, swaying on the end of the two chains. The flog stung a little, but was not unbearable. The pain was less than the paddle she'd used on him that first day.

The flog swung in again, this time cracking down against his abdomen.

Peter felt a bizarre sense of martyrdom, and a black-edged masochistic pleasure began to infiltrate his thoughts. The big vibrator was still stuffed deep inside his rectum, buzzing away, and his cock remained fully erect as the whip swung in again, then again, then again, the sound of its impact filling the room as it cut into his abdomen and chest.

His skin began to colour pink, then grow red, as stinging pain spread over his body. Kathleen swung the whip harder, and he gasped as it stung, especially when the strips cracked down around his nipples. She stepped closer, wrapping her fingers around the shaft of his erection and pumping it a few times. He groaned involuntarily and the crowd laughed.

Then she was gone, and after a long moment he realised she was behind him. The whip sailed in and lashed the small of his back, and he cried out again, more startled than in pain. The blows began to land steadily, Kathleen moving the whip up and down the length of his back, but ignoring his buttocks.

She paused and came forward, and he felt her grip the vibrator. She pumped it slowly in and out, and he was somewhat surprised to see how easily it moved now, and how deeply it penetrated without pain. She was able to force the entire thing into his rectum so that his anus closed behind it.

Then she resumed her whipping, his back soon burning as she swung the flog with strength and determination.

Then she paused, and he waited, breathless, gasping, his body filled with a strange sexual tension. His insides were quivering around the vibrator, his cock painfully erect. And he found himself wanting some new degradation, wanting the crowd to watch his further humiliation.

The whip swung overhand now, and came down between his legs. The bulk of the long strands of leather struck down against his slightly puckered anal opening and the flesh of his buttocks and inner thighs. But the ends swung down and in to strike at his testicles and cock where they hung below, and he squealed in pain, jerking and twisting violently.

The crowd laughed and applauded as Peter gasped in shock. Then the whip landed again and once more he yelped and jerked, his hands pulling instinctively against the restraints, as if trying to rise up and protect himself. The flog landed again, and again, and he twisted and yelped and thrashed as the stinging, aching force of the impact made his testicles swell and burn with pain, and his erection scream and bounce wildly.

Two more women moved to stand on either side of him, each holding a flog. Then one began to whip his chest, belly and abdomen while the other swung her whip against his back, shoulders and buttocks. Kathleen continued to swing her flog overhand, and it continued to crack down between his legs.

The rapid blows of pain momentarily struck him dumb, then he began yelping and crying out, twisting and jerking, straining at his bonds, writhing and shaking as his entire body was stabbed by flickering needles of pain. His muscles jerked and spasmed and his mind spun in helpless confusion and shock.

And yet in the midst of it his arousal somehow remained. He was aware, at his core, that he was nude, splayed open before a crowd of people, and that the outrage being done him was unbelievably lewd and shockingly perverse. And as the strips of leather snapped at his testicles and the head of his cock he felt a tremendous surge of lust and sensual heat envelop him. Once again he felt the masochistic martyr-like pleasure, and then even a strange exhibitionistic glory at being the lewd focus of so much attention.

Kathleen stopped, and he felt her fingers probing just within his anus. She pulled on the vibrator, slowly easing it up and out. His anus remained briefly open, then another, even larger vibrator was pressed against it. He heard the murmurs of awe from the crowd as his anus began to sting from the force of its insertion. The vibrator, more powerful than the previous ones, felt like it was tearing him open, and he groaned loudly as Kathleen forced it in, crying out as it stabbed deep inside him and his insides twisted and protested.

The whipping continued, and he twisted and writhed, crying out again and again, half-mad now as the crowd moved in closer to watch.

After an endless period of near agony the whipping stopped. He felt the vibrator begin to pump in and out, pumping freely despite its thickness. A hand gripped the base of his shaft and began to squeeze rhythmically, in tandem with the pumping of the vibrator. He felt a tremendous pressure in his groin, a tremendous heat, and then a climax rolled over him like a tidal wave, swamping his mind and senses and sending his body into convulsions.

His back arched again and again, and the crowd cheered and applauded as semen began to spatter down to the floor in front of him. Each beat of his heart was accompanied by a squeeze of his shaft and a hard, cruel thrust of the dildo, and another powerful spurt of semen flew out to spatter against the floor at the feet of the crowd.

CHAPTER NINE

"Put these on."

Jeffrey looked up as the black woman flung him his clothes. He stared at her in confusion, then stared again as she tossed him the key to the restraints around his ankles. She left the room and for long moments he looked at the clothes and keys, wondering if it was a trick.

Yet he'd been told he could do what he wanted, so there should be no punishment.

Not that the bitch, beautiful as she was, needed any excuse to punish him.

He dressed slowly, certain that at any minute she would return, and then mockingly demand he strip before punishing him.

With his shoes on he began to feel more like a man again, and wondered if he dared go to the door and try the knob. The door opened and she gestured him forward, then turned her back.

He followed her down a small hall and into another room. There was a chair there, and a television. She pushed him into the chair.

"Sit," she said.

Then she turned on the television and left.

He hissed as he saw the pictures which came onto the screen. It was him, naked. And it only got worse. He cringed as he watched himself being lewdly sexually abused, treated like a dog, like an animal. He watched and listened to himself grovel before the women, licking their feet and pleasing them sexually. He watched the black woman rape him with the dildo, then watched himself masturbating with and without a hood.

The black woman returned, smirking. "We thought we'd

give you enough evidence to take to the police. We just knew how outraged you were and how much you wanted to get back at us."

Jeffrey did not speak. He was too appalled to speak, and too afraid of the woman in any event.

She went to the machine and took out the tape, then handed it to him.

"A souvenir. Of course we have more copies. But we knew you'd want one for yourself. Feel free to show it to anyone you want."

With that she hauled him to his feet and marched him into a garage. She demanded he get down on the floor of his own Porsche, and then she got into the driver's seat and drove out of the garage.

"It's been fun, Jeffrey, and I know you've enjoyed yourself," she said, smirking down at him. "I'm sure you realise by now that telling anyone what happened would not only humiliate you in front of the police, but that this tape, and others, would have to be played out for the court. Can you imagine what the tabloids would do with a story like this? You'd be on the front page of every newspaper in the country for weeks on end."

She smiled and shook her head. "Certainly sell a lot of newspapers, and make your company famous."

She laughed to herself at the look on his face, and then put a finger to her lips.

"If you don't tell, neither will we," she said tauntingly.

Then the car stopped. She blew him a kiss, got out, and slammed the door behind her.

Jeffrey remained on the floor for a long minute before finally climbing back onto the seat. He saw that he was in the company parking lot, and was alone. He stared down at the tape, then began to tremble and shake. He felt rage and frustration grip him amid a wash of relief. Yet at the back of his mind was a small stab of regret. He hated them. Vile, filthy bitches, but he knew that a part of him had responded enthusiastically to their dark cruelty, and felt a certain knowledge that he would have to seek out something similar to satisfy the urges they had awakened.

He got into the driver's seat and shifted into gear, then turned the car around and headed for his flat. There was no question of going to the authorities, of course. But somehow, some way, he would find out who they were and he would get back at the two of them.

***

Peter moaned dazedly as a sharp stinging pain swept him out of the half-conscious haze. His eyes fluttered weakly, and another sharp stinging - in his cheek - made him cry out. A hand gripped his hair and pulled his head up and back.

He recalled very little of the events of the previous evening. In truth, he recalled very little about who he was. He was still very hazy, his head throbbing dully. His body stung front and back, and there was a particular ache around his groin.

Peter was hanging by his ankles, but not vertically. His arms had been pulled together behind his back, so tightly together his elbows were touching and his shoulders ached dully. His wrists were also bound together, and pulled up and back, serving to arch his body up and back towards where his ankles were chained to a low bar.

His testicles were purplish red, for a leather strap was pulled tightly around his cock at its base, and a chain was hung with weights below it, pulling the strap down, putting pressure on his balls. A vibrator was stuffed deep into his rectum, serving to keep his insides quivering and twisting and a pair of headphones was taped over his ears.

Soft music played over the headphones, and along with it

were voices, stern female voices mixed with a male voice which was respectful and timid. The voices spoke of obedience and service, of the punishment which awaited disobedience and the pleasures of serving. He hardly heard the voices, or at least, paid them little attention. They were low, and he had to make an effort to actually understand them. And they had been playing for hours now, so that in his haze he was hardly aware of them.

The pressure was released from his testicles, and he felt an enormous sense of physical relief. Moments later a soft hand began to massage the head of his cock, which rapidly swelled as he became erect. The vibrator began to pump in and out of his rectum, and he quivered and moaned in nearly mindless pleasure.

Then it stopped, and the blindfold was pulled from his eyes. He found that he was staring into a naked female groin, but he did not know nor care who it belonged to. It was pushed forward and his tongue pushed out, almost instinctively, and began to lick. His scalp stung somewhat as whoever it was held his head level, but he paid that little heed. There were worse aches in his body, and he knew he must perform properly or face more.

As he began to lick the vibrator began to pump in his rectum again, and he once again moaned in pleasure. His cock throbbed and he felt his hips quiver with the urge to thrust himself into something soft and moist and tight.

He satisfied the woman, and the vibrator was pushed back, then he felt himself being slowly lowered to the floor. He felt an exquisite sense of relief as the pressure was finally released from his arms and legs and shoulders, and no little of this sensory delight transmitted itself to his groin. He began to grind himself against the hard stone beneath his body.

***

The shelves which lined the walls of the office were of stainless steel. There were no books on them. Instead they were crowded with figurines and statues, games and knick-knacks, pictures and high-tech toys. Jeffrey sat behind a desk, which was a good six feet long, and almost as wide. It was made of glass and supported by a stainless steel framework. There were two computer screens under the glass, and a built in keyboard, which could be accessed simply by sliding a small 'window' aside.

Jeffrey Fitzwilliams sat behind the desk in a large leather chair, licking his lips nervously while doing his best to appear calm to the man across the desk from him.

"And you have no idea where they live or who they might work for?" the man asked.

"I've said as much," Jeffrey replied curtly.

The man had come highly recommended. He was a private investigator, and a discreet one, who did a great deal of work for London's high technology companies. Of course, Jeffrey had not told him why he was looking for two women named Yvette and Kathleen. That was the good thing about hiring people. They did as one told them and could not demand answers one did not wish to give. He had described Yvette and Kathleen fairly well, and told the man that one or both had to be working in the field of high technology. He had also told the man that they had stolen information from his company - which was true enough.

"There are damn few women in this sector who look like them," he told the man. "Anyone who has encountered either, at a conference, a trade show, or during at a gathering of some kind or another, would remember them. And you have no idea how they accessed this information?"

Jeffrey frowned. The man was proving to be somewhat irritating in the way he continued to rephrase questions Jeffrey had already refused to answer.

"No."

"How do you know they have it?"

"I know."

The man sighed, and Jeffrey's frown deepened. The man was going to be taking his money and ought to simply do as Jeffrey told him. He wondered if his contact had given him the wrong name. This man with his cheap suit and square, blocky head could hardly have the brains to investigate something properly. On top of that he was Irish!

"You see, Mr. Fitzwilliams, the fastest way to discover who these women are would be to find out what their connection is to your company. That is to say, find out how they learned of the existence of this information and how they purloined it. If they dealt with one of your employees, for example, bribed or blackmailed one..."

"I realise this might make the investigation somewhat more difficult," Jeffrey said stiffly. "However, I am told you are an excellent investigator."

His tone made it clear he was beginning to doubt his information.

"Well, just so long as you're aware that setting these restrictions will make the job more difficult."

"Can you or can you not find them?"

The man paused a moment as if thinking. "Likely I can," he said. "As you say, they sound like an unusual pair. Even individually there aren't many like them among the pocket protector set."

Jeffrey glared at him and the man cleared his throat, as if realising he was talking to a member of that "set".

"Very well then. I shall expect results, and quickly. Keep me informed of what progress you make and..."

"Uh, Mr. Fitzwilliams."

Jeffrey frowned again.

"You see, given the information you've given me, or that

you haven't, I should say, my only chance of finding them is by going around and asking. That means there's not likely to be any progress to make until I run across someone who recognises the description. At that point I'll find the person, take a picture, and bring it back to you so you can verify it's them."

"Very well," Jeffrey said testily.

The man rose and Jeffrey rose as well, coming around his desk to shake the man's hand. It irritated him that the detective was so much larger than he was. The man was taller, had a powerful chest, wide shoulders, and a strong, work-roughened hand which virtually swallowed his own soft pale fingers.

It was absurd that he should feel jealous of this big, stupid, thuggish man! He was a wealthy, powerful executive, a millionaire well respected in his industry. This character was a low-level type who probably drove an ancient creaking car he could barely afford to keep fuelled.

And yet, because of his size he probably had women throwing themselves at him everywhere he went. He'd probably had more beautiful women than Jeffrey had had haircuts. It wasn't fair!

If he'd had a body like this man's those bitches wouldn't have been able to kidnap and humiliate him. The shoe would have been on the other foot!

Jeffrey saw the man out, then went back to his desk imagining Kathleen and Yvette on their knees before him, chained and beaten down, whimpering for his forgiveness as they sucked on his erection.

Bitches.

He glanced at the television in the corner, knowing the tape was locked securely in his desk and wondering if he had time to look at it again. He had watched it so often since they had released him that he had it memorised; yet he could not keep from looking at it again and despite his anger as he watched himself being degraded and demeaned his cock persisted in becoming erect each time he watched the black woman raping him.

Not that he thought of it that way, of course. Only women could be raped.

But each time Jeffrey watched the tape which showed her using him his cock became erect again, and he fantasised about being on his knees with his bottom raised, or hanging from his wrists, or standing impaled on the long upright bar.

He masturbated several times a day now, and he used a dildo he had bought over the internet, too shamed to buy it in person, used it to pretend he was a prisoner again, and that a beautiful woman was using him like an animal.

He would teach them. He would punish them for making him into what he was, for giving him these filthy fantasies and making him feel like less than a man. He would show them all just what a man could do! Oh yes!

***

Collin Butler wandered down the hall from Fitzwilliams' office, eyeing the well-dressed types around him scurrying about like rats, and made a face. What a life, he thought. He got into one of the elevators; the walls, like much else in this building, of mirror-finished stainless steel, and rode back downstairs. The elevator stopped several times along the way, and as the doors opened he caught glimpses of the fabric-covered cubicles where the computer engineers and programmers worked.

Just like rats, he thought to himself. What a sad way to spend your life.

No doubt they made a lot more money than him, had nicer flats and cars, and bigger bank accounts - with stock options.

But what good did it do them all? They spent all their lives working, gazing at a computer screen, fiddling with software and attending meetings. Gah!

Collin had worked on the docks when he was younger, which wasn't a bad life at all. You worked with your mates, moved around a lot, dressed as you liked, were able to laugh and joke with people, and stopped off at the pub afterwards to laugh and joke some more. If you were lucky, and Collin was often lucky, you left with a pretty thing under your arm for some more of what life had to offer.

What kind of a man would replace that with working ten or twelve hours a day before a computer in a little box with a boss glaring at him any time he dared to try and talk to someone?

He left the building and paused on the pavement to pull a stick of gum from his pocket, unwrap it, and slide it into his mouth. He was fairly sure this Fitzwilliams fellow had encountered these women personally in some capacity he didn't want to talk about. Likely they'd rolled him in some way, come onto him, pushing their tits in his face, then drugged him and stolen the data somehow. No doubt that was why he was too embarrassed to talk about it. Poor little bastard was probably a virgin.

So, how was he going to find these women? Perhaps they were in the industry, but then again another company might simply have hired them. In that case his searching for them at other high tech companies was going to be a waste of time. He'd be better off searching the bars.

Collin knew the high tech community well, for it was quite insular, and one recommendation followed another, leading him from job to job within the "community". And the truth was that tall blondes were not all that memorable outside of the geeky world of high technology. Even there they were becoming more and more common as marketing departments realised that the best people to sell products to nerdish computer fanatics were beautiful young women.

The black woman, however, might be more of a standout. If she really was a bodybuilder, well, there weren't that many female bodybuilders, and even fewer of those were black. And most of those were lesbians, which meant they usually had quite short hair. A black female bodybuilder with cornrows down to her bottom would stand out rather well.

Collin had a soft spot for big, strong women. He'd had numerous women in his life, from the tiny, flirty, girlish sort, to those who'd have done well on a man's rugby team. All in all, he preferred a woman with some strength to her, both inside and out. He was a big, strong man and liked his women to be similar.

What, he wondered, had the black woman done to that pretty little man inside? He smiled at the thought, then found his car, and headed across town. There were a couple of local magazines which covered the bodybuilding scene, and if the black woman had ever competed there'd likely be pictures of her. That, he thought, would be a blessing. If he could find the girl the same afternoon he could take a few days off to work on other cases, and the rich boy wouldn't even know enough to complain.

Technically, he supposed that was a little dishonest. But overcharging snotty rich boys did not strike him as being particularly immoral. Fitzwilliams wouldn't miss it and Collin could use the money. He wondered what Fitzwilliams intended doing once he found the girl, though. He clearly had no desire to involve the authorities. He gave a mental shrug. He wasn't being paid to worry about such things.

***

Kathleen went to SpecterWare to prod the engineers who

were examining "her" new designs and trying to work a few kinks out of them. There was still one major difficulty with implementing the system, a difficulty that the people at Ecom hadn't been able to figure out.

This was very irritating, because if they figured it out before her own people did they could still announce their product before she did and all her work would go for nothing. She sat at her desk, pondering the problem for some time. It wasn't as if this idea was entirely unique, and there were any number of companies quite similar to Ecom who had a habit of exploring interesting new research. It was not only possible but, in fact, likely, that several other companies were working on aspects of this problem at that very moment.

Not that any of them would make that information public.

There was one organisation a high-tech firm would talk to about their research, however, and that was their banker if they needed a loan. Many, if not most of the newer, high flying tech companies had little income and gained their research and operating money either through the stock market, private venture capitalists, or...... banks.

Linda Tarlington worked in a bank. In fact, she worked in the commercial loans section of Batherby's Bank, which had been doing everything it could to ingratiate itself into the good books of the growing high technology community in hopes of growing along with it. Linda would know where she needed to focus her attention.

But Linda was a bitch, and while she didn't precisely dislike Kathleen she certainly wasn't fond of her. On the other hand, Linda did admire innovation, especially in terms of boy toys. Linda was a member of the Black Oyster club, which was cutting edge leather at its most hip in fashion, and a raving lesbian who loved nothing better than seeing men degraded.

Kathleen thought about that silly toy Yvette had been working on for the past few months, the one she'd experimented on Charles with. That was just the sort of idiotic, but clever thing which would delight Linda. Especially since it could, with very little adaptation, be used by women as well as men.

And Peter had done so well in his little public showing the other day. No doubt he would delight in another. She would stop off at Charles' office first, and then go home and prepare Peter for another interesting night.

***

"You have a visitor, Mr. Evans-Finch," the girl said.

He looked up sharply. "I'm not to be disturbed," he snapped.

"She insisted, sir," the girl said nervously.

Charles looked past the young woman and the inhaled sharply as Kathleen walked through the door.

"Very well," he said, waving the girl off.

Kathleen smiled and closed the door behind her, and he slid out of his chair and onto his knees, his heart pounding.

"Mistress!"

"Charles, my sweet little pet. Are we busy today?"

"Never too busy for you, mistress."

"Expecting company soon?"

"No mistress."

"Strip then."

He hesitated, then, his fingers trembling, he stood and quickly removed his expensive jacket, draping it across the back of his leather and steel executive chair. He untied his shoes and slipped them off, then placed his socks inside them. Straightening once more, he loosened and removed his tie, unbuttoned his shirt, and stripped them off. Finally he undid his belt, opened his trousers, and shoved them down his legs, along with his shorts. Naked, he stood up and faced her, already erect, face flushed with excitement.

His eyes darted to the door with a touch of nervousness.

"Have you been doing as you promised?"

"Yes, Mistress! Every chance I get I let people know about SpecterWare and what a good buy it is!"

"Sweet boy," she purred, moving forward and sliding her fingers through his hair.

She pulled on a tuft of hair, forcing him to his feet, then pushed him back against his chair so that he sat down heavily.

"Spread your legs, my little slut," she ordered. "More. Drape them over the arms of your chair."

She smiled when he complied, then opened her bag and drew out a long strap. She wrapped one end around his left leg just above the knee, drew it down beneath the chair, and up the opposite side to wrap around his right leg in an identical manner. Then, with Charles co-operating, she strapped his wrists together over his head, leading that strap down over the backrest to lock around the base of the chair.

"Now, Charles, I must say that I do appreciate your helping us along in this way," she said, propping her bottom on his desk, "but I am somewhat disappointed that you've been unable to come up with more information on the research efforts of our competitors."

"I'm trying mistress," he exclaimed, "But they like to keep those things as close to the chest as possible until they're almost ready to release them."

'Officially, yes. But unofficially, you can bring some of their bright young men out for long lunches, can you not, and ply them with liquor and compliments?"

"But they wouldn't have specifications, mistress..."

"If I have some idea of who is working on what I can use

other methods to look deeper," she said, resting her high-heeled foot in his lap.

"Yes mistress!" he panted.

She raised her foot, pressing the heel against his chest, digging it in as he clenched his teeth in pain.

"You do want to help me, don't you, Charles?" she asked in a sad voice.

"Anything mistress! You know that!" he gasped.

"But you're not doing everything you could."

"I'm sorry mistress! I'll do more," he promised.

She smiled, and then drew a small, black metal box from her purse. There were two metal spikes at one end, each about one inch long, and three inches apart, and when she pressed a button on the device a crackling arc of electricity leapt between them. She bent and scooped up Charles' shorts, then shoved them into his mouth.

"Just to recall to you the urgency of your work," she said, smiling.

She let the end of the box slide down between Charles' thighs, ensured that the two spikes bracketed his erection, and pressed the button.

Charles' body shook and thrashed violently, and Kathleen watched entranced, her own pussy growing hot and liquid at the sight of him. She pressed the button again, watching the crackling arc of electricity join his purplish red erection, watching his member jump, and his body writhe. Again, and again, and again she pressed down on the button, finally holding it in place, as he seemed to go mad, threatening to tear free of the straps.

The battery wore out all too quickly and she placed the device back into her purse. Charles continued to tremble and shake, his limbs spasming and twitching as he lay there. He was drooling slightly, his eyes glazed. Kathleen felt a surge of power and exultation at her ability to so control and so punish a man.

She looked down and saw that his erection was still quite firm. She smiled, reaching for it, taking it into her hands and caressing it. She rarely did so, but just this once, with Charles hardly aware of what was happening, she dropped to her knees before him and took his cock into her mouth. She felt again the power she had over him, wondered anew at how influence over this small bit of flesh could so control a man, and began to suck.

She bobbed her lips up and down, kissed, licked, and massaged his member, and it soon erupted, emptying itself into her mouth, giving of itself, to shrivel up in exhaustion.

Just like men did, she thought, pleased.

CHAPTER TEN

The device Yvette had worked on, and which Kathleen had teased her over, was, at its base, a simple child's wagon. Yvette had strengthened it, prettied it up, and added a soft cushioned bench and a place to put her feet, but in essence, it was still just a wagon. And Peter would pull it - on his hands and knees.

There was more to it than that, of course, as Peter soon discovered. Kathleen fitted a harness tightly around his torso. Thick straps went over his shoulders, criss-crossed his chest, and tightly circled his hips. A final strap descended from his the waist belt at front and back, and met up between his legs. There was a hole through which his cock descended and another hole over his anus. The straps were then tightly buckled together. The short cable pulling the wagon was then attached to a ring directly between his anus and cock.

But, of course, there was more. The reins she used to guide him went through rings set in the sides of the strap around his waist, and then to a bit forced between his jaws. Two long metal poles extended forward from the wagon. One ended in a soft, spongy plastic dildo a good foot long. This was in turn, thrust deep into Peter's rectum. The second ended in a hollow tube, the inside of which was lined with soft silk. This was fitted over the head of his cock before being strapped in place.

Crawling was not a graceful method of movement, nor fluid, nor smooth. A crawling man must move one knee forward through the air, lay it down, pause to take his weight upon that knee, then raise the opposite knee and swing it forward in turn, to then pause and repeat the process. During each pause he was, essentially, immobile for perhaps half a second of time before the second knee pulled him forward once more. It was a lurching sort of movement and the genius of the dildo and the tube was that it accounted for that, and also for the fact that the wagon was under no such limitation. The wagon, on wheels, had no need to pause. Once pulled into motion it would continue to roll until it lost momentum.

As Sir Isaac Newton once theorised, an object in motion tends to stay in motion until acted upon by some external force. In this case, the wagon continued in motion until the dildo at the end of its handle thrust itself so deep within Peter's rectum that it could go no further. And the end of the hollow tube - strapped to his groin, slid fully forward over his cock - so long as it was erect.

Peter did not realise this at first, when he knelt obediently and was hooked up to the wagon. He realised it almost at once, however, as he began to pull the wagon up the narrow hallway under Kathleen's command. Each time he moved forward he pulled away from the wagon, and the cable permitted this, permitted him to move far enough for the dildo to slide down his rectum so that it was nearly withdrawn.

Likewise the soft, slightly too thin tube slid back until only the head remained within. Then as he paused to swing his opposite knee forward, the wagon, which he had set in motion, caught up to him, the dildo thrusting deep into his belly again so as to cause him to grunt at the strength of its thrust. The tube too slid fully down the length of his erection. Swinging forward his opposite knee and moving away would then pull him halfway off the dildo once again, and slide his cock back up the length of the silky tube. Then, inevitably, as he shifted to his other knee, the wagon would catch up and the same events would repeat.

The faster he crawled, the more momentum was imparted to the wagon. The more momentum the wagon had the harder the dildo was thrust into his bottom and the harder his cock was thrust down the silky tube. Kathleen was delighted with the look of the new toy, having paid it little attention when Yvette was putting it together. It was deliciously garish and crude. Linda would love it. Of course, Peter needed a little more of a costume to make it right. She placed a head harness on him and buckled it into place, then fastened two high, plumed feathers to opposite sides just over the ears. She carefully painted his finger and toenails, and then put bright lipstick on his lips. She lifted both his ankles up and pressed them back against his buttocks. She then fitted a strong leather sleeve over them. The bottom of the sleeve, which fitted snugly against his knees, was padded, and this permitted him to crawl even on stone without causing him any damage.

She liked her toys pretty, not scratched or scraped up - unless, of course, she chose to put the marks on them herself.

With him prepared she dressed herself, wearing an extremely tight red Lycra dress which had quite a high hemline that stopped just short of her crotch. The sides of the dress consisted of nothing but thin straps and the front plunged to bare half her breasts, the thin, straining cups held together by little more than tiny side straps.

She had Peter load the wagon into her car, and then climb in himself, already fully "dressed" for the evening. Peter was quite nervous yet oddly, even unbound he did not even really consider refusing her orders. It did not occur to him to simply cast off the gear she had put on him, find clothing and walk away. It wasn't that he was looking forward to whatever Mistress Kathleen had in store for him that night, for in fact he was not. But his mind, already weak and pliable, had been so conditioned to obedience that anything else was simply unthinkable. Literally.

So, naked in all respects which mattered, he climbed into the car beside the wagon and sat quietly as she shut the door then moved up to the front and started the engine.

"Remember," she said, looking at him in the rear view mirror, "I expect absolute obedience from you. If you embarrass me by acting like a silly baby and refusing to do what you ought I will be very, very cross."

"Yes, mistress," he said nervously.

He saw little beyond the back of her head and the traffic in front of the car as she drove to the club, for the side windows were darkly tinted. Then the car pulled into a lane and came out in a small, sheltered lot just behind the club. Kathleen parked next to the rear entrance and came back to let him out. Peter looked around nervously at the open lot, for it was still quite bright enough out to light it up fully.

"Out!" she barked.

Wearing only the harness, he dropped from the van onto the hard packed earth of the rear lot. He found his cock beginning to swell at the excitement of being nude outdoors, but under her direction, turned quickly and lifted down the wagon, then placed the two knee sleeves onto it and rolled it forward to the door. Kathleen rang the bell and a tall darkhaired woman in a leather jump suit opened it, smiling at her, then at Peter.

"Well, well, who's this?" she asked sweetly. "New toy?"

"Very new," Kathleen said proudly.

She snapped her finger at him and he hurriedly pushed the wagon inside.

"What is this?" the woman asked.

"You'll see. Is Linda here?"

"Of course. She wouldn't miss tonight."

Once inside Kathleen had him kneel and put the sleeves over his legs, then strapped him to the wagon, explaining to the woman how it worked. The woman laughed in delight at the explanation of the dildo and sleeve, especially as Kathleen tried to explain its effects scientifically, quoting Newton's first law of motion.

"I bet old Sir Isaac never tried to use such an example to demonstrate," she chortled.

Kathleen grinned smugly, then climbed into the wagon and sat down, taking up the reins.

"This should be good," the woman said with a broad grin.

She hurried ahead to open up doors, and Kathleen picked up a long buggy whip and slashed it down lightly across Peter's bare rump.

"Onward, dog!" she called.

And so he crawled forward, grunting each time the dildo drove itself up into his belly, turning a corner, going through a door held open by the woman, then another into a large room filled with milling people. Many of the people were dressed as Kathleen was, while others were dressed - or undressed - much the same way he was.

But his face flushed as so many eyes turned their way, and then cheers started up from the viewers as Kathleen lashed his buttocks again, ordering him to move faster. Moving faster, of course, meant the wagon moved faster, and that the dildo plunged even harder into his rectum each time he shifted knees. It also had his cock sliding furiously up and down the silk-lined tube. That, along with the steady, hard plunging of the dildo in his rectum was starting to make him quiver with sexual excitement.

Being the centre of such lewd attention was not as shocking or humiliating, as it had been the first time around, and, in truth, he felt less exposed on his hands and knees.

The crowd laughed and cheered, clearing aside as he crawled quickly forward, pulling Kathleen's wagon. She tugged on the left rein, and he turned left, more people pulling back out of his way with grins, smirks or other signs of appreciative amusement. The buggy whip cut down onto his back, but lightly, and he tried to crawl faster still.

He made a circuit of a large, dimly lit, high-ceilinged room and then stopped before a bar, where Linda climbed out of her chair and bowed to the applause of the crowd. Enthusiastic people crowded around, all congratulating her on her entrance, and her fine beast of burden. She acted modestly and generously allowed others to take turns on her new vehicle. Peter had to make several more circuits of the room, then, bearing both men and woman around, getting more and more aroused as the dildo pounded into his bottom and the sleeve slid up and down over his cock.

When Kathleen finally un-harnessed him from the wagon, it was to collar him, and lead him further around the room on all fours, as she paused to meet and talk with people he was ordered to lick at their boots or toes to show his obedience and submissiveness. Peter felt somewhat dazed by it all, but had slipped into a mental role whereby it was all proper and oddly natural. And so his arousal continued, mixed with a strange feeling of freedom and only a little shame.

"A good place for them all."

Kathleen turned and smiled at a thin, dark-haired women with a narrow, angular face.

"Linda, my dear," she said smugly.

"Interesting little wagon you have," the woman said. "I can see how it could be adapted to good use with my precious."

Kneeling at her feet was a bald headed girl who looked barely over eighteen. She had enormous breasts for her size and they hung below her as she crawled. Linda held a leash which was hooked to a thick ring set in the centre of the girl's nose. Two small bells were attached to rings set in her nipples, and they chimed lightly as she moved.

"Yes, and of course, you can alter the size of the er, insertion," Kathleen said, giving the woman, and then the girl, significant looks.

"It's you bisexual types who worry about size," the woman sniffed.

"Of course." Kathleen chose not to mention the chest implants Linda had given her pet.

"Actually, I must confess the idea for this was Yvette's."

"Oh? And where is Sheba of Africa these days?"

"Stripping at a night club for the benefit of slobbering men."

Linda's lip curled in distaste.

"She likes the money, and the way the men drool and beg."

"Men are a waste of time." She looked at Peter. "Except, perhaps, as beasts of burden."

"Of course. You know, Linda, I've been meaning to get together with you for some time."

"Oh?"

"Yes, you know, Yvette is so hard to please sometimes. I was hoping perhaps you might know a trick or two." She raised her eyebrows and smiled, and Linda smirked. "I know more than a thing or two, dear."

She looked at Peter again and sneered.

"Why don't we go somewhere more quiet. You can chain your pet up somewhere or give him to some slut to play with."

"An excellent suggestion."

Peter was quite alarmed, at first, when Kathleen handed his leash over to a strange woman and then left the room. Yet his anguish slowly gave way to an even deeper sense of arousal. For now, with a number of smirking, dark-eyed women surrounding him, all strangers, he knew true degradation. They made obscene comments about him and forced him to position his body in lewd and vulnerable ways.

He was slapped, strapped, pinched, had his hair pulled, and his face shoved into the groins of several women, who he was forced to please with his rapidly tiring tongue and jaw. Then they brought over a slave girl, a quite pretty one, who, he gathered, was the property of one of the women. The girl was a lesbian and could not abide men, and for that reason, to punish and degrade her, she was forced to kneel before Peter and offer up her sex to him.

She was clearly disgusted and appalled, trembling with the desire to flee, but like him, she obeyed her commands. And when Peter was ordered to mount her he did so with great enthusiasm, in some sense delighting, along with the watching women in her revulsion as he thrust himself deep into her tight sex and began to ride her.

All in all, it was a rather exciting night for Peter, and he was almost sorry to see it end, to crawl back to Kathleen's car and be driven home.

***

The next day he was at work as if nothing had happened, feeling a delicious sense of secrecy around his colleagues, wondering smugly what they would think if they could have seen him the previous evening.

Peter found the work at Jentech to be quite interesting. The engineers there were really on the cutting edge, and had a great deal of enthusiasm for their upcoming projects. Of course, these projects were secret, but engineers weren't very good at keeping secrets, and liked to brag. It took very little time, a matter of days, for him to get a good grasp of what Jentech was doing which might be useful to Specterware.

There was, in fact, a significant program already completed and in the hands of their marketing people which would, when released, greatly affect the sales of SpecterWare's own software. It was better, faster, and more powerful than what SpecterWare had to offer. SpecterWare's stock would take a beating when it was announced.

He thought briefly about forgetting it. He thought about the sneer on Kathleen's face as Yvette punished him and the way she made him grovel before her. There wasn't time to steal the information anyway, and he would immediately be suspect if their program turned up at SpecterWare. Yet Kathleen would thank him for helpful information like this, perhaps she'd even let him have sex with her!

He reached for the phone and called her office, but got no answer. Muttering, he hung up, wondering what he should do next. Likely Kathleen would want to know everything about this new program, how it could be accessed, how long before it was released and such. So he set about learning everything he could about it.

That was surprisingly easy. To start with the computer refused to tell him anything about the project. But since he had the project number, the file handling system was pleased to tell him where in the computer, information about the new project was stored. He had a brief thought that he could, with a little effort, erase every trace of the project.

That would do little good, though. There was certainly information on the personal computers of the people involved, and there had to be printed material, backup diskettes and such. He'd have to actually go to where the engineers worked and erase those disks and drives. And someone would certainly tap him on the shoulder while he was doing so and ask what in hell he thought he was doing.

No, the idea was silly. He'd tell Kathleen, though, and let her decide what to do about it.

***

Kathleen examined her stocks with a pleased smile on her face. The stock kept rising and rising, and her little investment kept growing and growing. She moved from one stock listing group to another, looking at their recommendations to buy SpecterWare, their speculations about how well the stock was likely to do in the future, and then examined the charts which showed the sharp upward climb of the stock's price.

Charles was out gathering information for her, as was Yvette, as was Peter, and Linda had given her a number of sources where she could find more.

Life was good.

The phone rang and she answered it with a happy tone to her voice, then frowned as she realised it was Peter. She had told him not to call her, just in case his new employers were monitoring phone calls. Her irritation, however, soon turned to anger and frustration. If the new product he told her about was released it would certainly damage SpecterWare's stock price. Jentech was a direct competitor. A better product in this area would take market share away from SpecterWare. If their stock fell by ten percent she would get a margin call from her broker, and then she'd be in deep trouble.

"Damn! Damn! Damn!" she cursed.

"I'm sorry mistress," he said in a pathetic voice.

"Shut up you idiot and let me think."

She glared at the wall, her expression set and harsh.

"I'll get back to you."

She hung up and cursed aloud again.

Why did they have to pick now to come out with this new product?

She paced back and forth, wondering what, if anything, could be done.

If she could stop the product from being released, or at least delay it for a while - but how to do that?

Like Peter, she considered destroying the information at Jentech, and like him she almost immediately discarded the idea as impractical. It would be in several locations, with backup diskettes.

But desperate times called for desperate measures.

If Peter worked late at the office he might be able to sneak her in. Perhaps she could then get to the areas where the information was kept and manually delete everything she found. A good, solid magnet would destroy the hard drives of the personal computers, along with any diskette's nearby, an that would leave the main computer - and whatever paper files she found. Shredders might do for them.

Ridiculous. Yet she had no choice. She couldn't afford to have SpecterWare's stock dropping now.

Late at night, the place would be empty. Peter could stay late. There'd be security, of course, but they would be on predictable rounds, perhaps once hourly.

She picked up the phone and called Peter back, and he almost immediately came up with a problem.

"I thought of that, of course. The thing is, the doors to the separate sections are key coded. You can't get through without the proper card key. And once inside it's likely most of the information on their computers is duplicated on the director's computer. And he's in an actual office, like yours, with a door and a lock. Unless you plan on bashing down the door."

"Let me worry about that," she said in a chilly tone.

"Yes mistress," he replied not wanting to antagonise her.

"How late do most of the employees stay?"

"I'm not absolutely sure."

"Find out. How many security guards?"

"Well, er, just the one I think."

"Male, I trust?"

"Pardon? Oh, yes mistress."

"I can work with that," she said.

There was silence from the other end and she smiled to herself.

***

It was after ten in the evening when she and Yvette drove up and parked before the Jentech building.

"Do a good job, little slut, or else," Yvette purred.

"That's not amusing," Kathleen said in irritation.

Yvette laughed. "Well, do you think he'd believe I was Peter's wife?"

Kathleen glowered.

"You should have borrowed Linda's little pet."

"That girl would have frightened a fat-bellied security guard almost as much as you would."

"What makes you think he's fat?"

"Well, seated most of his working shift he's not likely to be a slim young Adonis, now is he?"

"Let's see, a miserable, low-paying job with miserable hours requiring no job skills except the ability to wear a polyester uniform. What kind of a specimen do you think is likely to hold down such a position?"

"You're being too hard on security guards. Some of them can even read and write."

Yvette snickered.

"Oh shut up," Kathleen growled.

She got out of the car, looking around, with a scowl. The outfit she had chosen to wear was not designed for modesty. The tight leather skirt barely covered her buttocks, and the blue, button-down blouse tucked into it was high enough, except that it was nearly completely sheer. Only the large pockets over her breasts were dark enough to shield what lay beneath. And she wore no bra.

She strolled up to the glass doors, and the brightly lit lobby beyond. The doors were locked, and she tapped lightly to attract the attention of the security guard sitting at his desk a dozen feet inside. The man looked up from a newspaper then jumped to his feet, hurrying forward to open the door.

He wasn't bad looking, at all, she thought. He was quite young, barely twenty, if that, but fairly well built, and could even be described as handsome.

"Yes?" he asked, eyes raking over her body and lingering on her breasts, savouring the hard points of her nipples as they pressed against the thin material.

Kathleen hated being looked at like that. It reminded her that so many men thought of her as little more than tits and ass. But she put a smile on her face regardless.

"I'm Gwendolyn Cross," she said sweetly. "I'm here to pick up my husband."

He stared at her chest lewdly "Certainly. Come on in"

She smiled at him again then walked past as he opened the door, brushing past and ensuring the briefest of contact with her elbow.

Of course, the blouse was completely sheer from the side, so he had an excellent view of the side of her breast as she moved slowly past. She walked up to his desk and he let the door close, following her slowly, eyes glued to her legs and bottom.

"Nice outfit," he said with a lewd grin.

"Thanks," she said, smiling modestly.

"I'll call your man."

"Thanks so much," she said, smiling again. She paused and turned, shifting her weight onto one leg so as to emphasise her figure.

He called Peter, never taking his gaze off her, eyes moving back and forth from her breasts to her thighs. By agreement, Peter asked to speak to "Gwen". The guard put her on the line and she smiled at him once again, ignoring his lewd stares.

"Hello?" she asked musically, a hint of mischief in her voice.

"Hello mistress. I hope you're not feeling too er, annoyed about this," he said hesitantly.

"Not at all."

The guard moved off to the side where he could stare at her breasts more easily, and she raised a hand, sliding fingers through her hair to give him a better look.

"I bet you look sexy right now."

"I certainly hope so."

"I wish it were me down there about to fuck you."

Her eyes widened and then narrowed. If he thought he was going to get away with that because he was out of range he was going to realise the error of his ways later on.

"I'm sure," she said, her voice now sounding cool.

"Well it's not fair," he whined.

So that was it. He was sulking because she was going to have sex with the guard. If he thought he had the slightest claim over her he was going to learn differently.

"You bastard," she said.

She hung up, looking irritated.

The guard looked up at her face and grinned. "Boy trouble?" he asked.

"He's going to be at least another hour. Can you believe that?" she demanded.

"Yeah, well you know these computer types," he said. "They work long hours. Don't seem to care for anything that isn't on a computer."

"Don't I know it!" she exclaimed.

She looked at his nametag. "Are you married, Earl?"

"Shit no."

"Huh. Maybe my miserable excuse for a husband will be saying the same soon. A girl needs some attention paid to her you know."

"Girl like you needs to get a lot of attention paid to her," he said with a lewd grin.

"If you were my boyfriend, Earl, would you rather stare at a computer screen or me?" she asked coyly.

"Shit lady, if you were mine I'd keep you naked and in bed all day long," he said, grinning again.

She turned to the side, looking around at the lobby, and letting his eyes stare at her full breasts. "Is there somewhere here I can wait?" she asked.

"No visitors are allowed after hours," he said.

She scowled. "Nobody will know, surely. Isn't there some... empty little room I can sit."

"Well... yes."

He crossed the lobby to the corridor, and then took what looked like a thick credit card and pushed it into a small slot next to a door. The door clicked, and he pushed it open, smiling at her. The office was small, with cabinets covering one wall, and a large desk most of the other.

"There's not much for you to do here," he said.

"Maybe I'll make my own entertainment," she said, sliding her tongue slowly along her lower lip.

His eyes widened and his tongue played out along his own lips.

"What do you do here at night by yourself, Earl?" she asked, sliding a finger along his chest.

"Fuck all, just a few patrols."

"That must get very... boring."

"Oh yes."

"I hate being bored, Earl," she said, giving him a soulful look and tilting her head mournfully to one side.

"Me too."

His hand went to her breasts and squeezed them both insolently, and then his lips came down harshly against her own as he pushed her back against the nearby wall.

"Not so hard," she protested as his fingers dug into the soft, tender flesh of her breasts.

"Tits like these need a good grope," he said, leering.

He half ripped her blouse to get it open, his big body crushing her back against the wall. Kathleen did not like being used like this, did not like being out of control, but on the other hand, he was occupied, which was what she wanted.

"Fucking hell," he groaned, taking a thick chunk of her breast into his mouth and sucking fiercely. "You need to get fucked raw!"

"Wait a minute," she gasped.

He reached between her legs and ripped her G-string off, tossing it behind him. His hands were rough as they raced over her body, squeezing her groin and buttocks, his teeth harsh on her breasts and lips.

She cursed softly, but managed to get a foot up behind him and pushed the door closed, noting the key card still in the lock. He never noticed.

***

Peter hurried across the lobby to the main doors and

opened one, waving. A moment later Yvette trotted up the steps and followed him inside.

"Where are they?" she whispered.

He beckoned across the lobby to the door he had seen them enter, and Yvette smiled, gently easing the key out of the lock.

There was a narrow, vertical window next to the door, and Peter stared through it, seeing his Kathleen propped against the desk, topless, kissing Earl. Her left foot was raised, propped on a bookshelf, and Earl's hand was between her thighs as they kissed, rubbing her pussy. He felt a sense of anger as he watched, wanting to go in and attack Earl, and then he looked suspiciously at her face, which seemed to be enjoying things far too much.

Yvette gripped his collar and yanked him back and they hurried across the lobby.

"Show me the way," she ordered.

Kathleen managed to push the guard back, and panted as he grinned at her.

"If you think you're going to back out now, you can forget it," he said with a sneer.

"Don't be ridiculous," she said. "I just want to see all of you. Get those clothes off."

Earl leered and yanked off his clip-on tie, then undid the top button of his shirt and peeled it up and over his head, tossing it behind him. He kicked off his shoes, then arrogantly undid his trousers and shoved them down and off. He wasn't wearing shorts.

He was a powerfully built man, she conceded. He didn't have the slim muscle definition of Peter or Charles, but he was a broad-shouldered young man in reasonable shape. And his cock was quite nicely sized.

"I'm gonna fuck your brains out," he promised, waggling his cock at her.

She grinned and backed off, manoeuvring him so that he was standing with his back to the side of the desk. Then she pushed him back hard so he fell over the desk, and climbed atop his body before he might think to twist free. He was surprised, and cursed for a moment, but when he found her straddling him he grinned anew, reaching up to grope her breasts with enough strength to make her wince.

"Fucking nice tits," he growled. "Cow tits, they are. And they need sucking!"

He yanked her down, his teeth gnawing at her nipples, his tongue lapping like a maddened dog, his mouth sucking loudly as she gasped and cursed. His hand slid down behind her, squeezing her bottom through the skirt, and then yanking the hem up to maul her bare flesh.

It took several minutes before she could pry herself free and sit up. Then, panting, she fought off his hands.

"Do you want to come inside me, Earl?" she asked.

"I want to come in you, on you and over you," he growled. "And after I fill that hot cunt of yours I'll spit in your ear and come down your throat."

He reached for her again but she drew back, still smiling. She reached down for her skirt and undid the belt around it, then drew the skirt up and off.

"Yeah. Show me what you got," he hissed, staring at her pussy. "Shaved! God, what a slut!"

"It's so my girlfriend can lick me more easily," she said.

As she'd known they would the words distracted him, and she was able to gather up the belt she'd put just beside her, slip the end through the buckle, and then swing it around in front of her without his noticing. Then she slid the loop over his wrists and yanked it tight.

He stared in surprise, not knowing what was happening, and she threw her weight forward, slamming his wrists down on the table above his head, his hands just over the edge.

There was a pipe running along the wall there, and she wrapped the belt quickly around it as he began to struggle.

"What the fuck... what are you fucking doing?" he demanded, wriggling.

"Are you a strong man, Earl?" she taunted.

She sat up, and he stared at her in confusion, still pulling at the belt.

"What kind of shit is this?"

She squeezed his erection, rose on her knees, and positioned it beneath her body, then sank down atop it, grunting in pleasure as it pushed deep into her moist pussy, filling her quite snugly.

"Yeah, that's nice," he groaned.

She stroked his chest with her hands, and then sat back.

"Earl's been a bad boy," she said teasingly. "What would Earl's boss think if he could see him like this?"

"Fuck me!" he demanded eagerly and thrust his hips up at her.

"Of course I will, Earl," she said smiling sardonically down at him.

She smiled. She reached past him and took a stapler off a counter, then opened it up. She squeezed it and a staple spat out to land atop his chest.

"Earl, Earl, Earl," she said with a smile. "Nothing in life comes free. And you really do need to learn to treat ladies with more respect."

"What?" his eyes widened in confusion, his expression matched them to show his lack of comprehension of her words.

She pressed the stapler against his chest and slapped her hand against the top. He screamed and jerked beneath him, and she laughed down at him.

"Fucking Christ!"

"It's only a staple, Earl," she teased. "Can't you take a

little pain?"

"Let me go, you mad bitch!"

She smiled again, and placed the stapler against his nipple, then slapped the top. Earl howled again, and her body jerked as he bucked wildly beneath her.

"Don't be such a baby Earl," she said reproachfully. "Big men can't go all to pieces over a couple of little staples."

He cursed her, and she slapped the stapler down again and again and again, and he howled, bucked and kicked his legs wildly as she laughed down at him.

She stapled her way up and down his chest, then moved downwards along his sides and belly. His legs started kicking and thrashing so she slipped off him, gathered a pair of electrical cords, and bound his ankles to the legs of the table, then she moved between his legs. He had gone soft, and she smiled up at him as she let the stapler slide over his groin.

"No! Don't! I'll fucking kill you!"

"Call me... mistress,' she said coyly.

"Fuck you!"

She closed the stapler drawing his soft cock between the base and the top.

"No! Mistress! Mistress!"

She smiled.

"You've gone all soft on me, Earl, and after promising me a good time too. That wasn't nice."

She opened the stapler again, then slapped it against his inner thigh and sent a staple deep into his flesh. He cursed and jerked, voicing his pain and hatred.

"If you'll make it up to me, Earl, perhaps we can find other uses for these staples."

She climbed atop him again, sliding slowly up his body. His chest was covered in staples now, and she raised her buttocks higher as she passed over it, then brought her sex down over his mouth.

"Let's see if you can do something useful with that foul mouth of yours, Earl," she said.

She gripped his hair in one hand and held the stapler up menacingly with the other, and Earl slowly began to lick.

"God. You're pathetic," she said, meaning it. "Are you a virgin?"

"I'm no fucking virgin!" he snarled as a muffled grunt.

"Well you certainly never seem to have put any effort into pleasing a woman before," Kathleen said. "But you're going to do it now."

She began to instruct him on how to perform to her satisfaction, and when he slowed he received a slap to the head, or in one instance, a staple through the earlobe that had him cursing non-stop for a full minute.

"You're such a delicate young man," Kathleen said.

She put a staple through his other ear, and giggled as he howled.

***

Peter and Yvette took the elevator upstairs and halted at the door to the corridor, which was locked. Yvette slipped the card into the slot, the door promptly unlocked, and they hurried inside.

"These are the cubicles of the people involved," Peter said, handing her the small list.

She nodded, and they moved towards them. When they arrived at the first one she dropped her bag, which thumped heavily onto a chair, and drew out a large square blocky machine. It had a cord attached, and she quickly plugged it in.

"Magnet," she said. "There's another in the bag. Take it out and go to the next office. Hurry it up. Even Kathleen won't be able to keep him occupied forever."

It took only minutes to run the magnets across the disks

stored in the offices and along the sides of the computers themselves. Yvette opened up the supervisor's offices then, for they did not know which was the right one, and she destroyed all the computer information stored within them. They then sifted through cabinet drawers in the offices and cubicles concerned, pulling out anything which seemed connected with the project and taking it up the hall to a large, industrial shredder.

The computer room was next. Peter had suggested he could do something through his own computer, but this left fewer traces. They used the magnets on the mainframe's storage disks, nearby racks of disks, and backup tapes. There wasn't time to find the right ones, so they simply ran the powerful magnets straight across every one.

Then, so that their visit would not be without profit, they crossed the building and copied all the information they could find on Jentech's artificial intelligence projects, and erased that as well.

All of it took considerably less than an hour. They hurried downstairs to find the lobby still empty, and went back to the office where Kathleen was occupying the guard.

"Oh! Ungh! Oh Christ! Fucking shit!"

Yvette smiled and Peter frowned.

They looked through the window to see the guard, naked, was lying on his back along the length of the desk, his legs hanging over one side, his wrists bound to a pipe on the other. His ankles were bound to the legs of the desk with electrical cord, and Kathleen was bent over above his groin.

Kathleen was naked as well, bent over his groin, bobbing her lips up and down on his purplish cock. As they watched she straightened up, smiled at him, drew her hand back, and slapped his erection hard.

Peter winced in sympathy and the man cursed in pain.

He watched her take him into her mouth again, then drew

back, held the tip of his cock with one hand, and slapped it hard once again.

"She certainly seems to be enjoying herself," Yvette observed.

"How do we let her know we're done?" Peter asked, frowning.

"Oh, it doesn't really matter."

"I'd like to leave," he said.

"Kathleen doesn't seem to be in a hurry."

He sulked, shifting the weight on his legs in his nervousness.

"Keep watch, and if she ever finishes playing, motion to her. I'm leaving. The two of you can take your car."

CHAPTER ELEVEN

Collin yawned just before picking up the phone. "Butler Consulting," he said in his best, most officious tone.

"Hello, Mr. Butler?"

"Yes. Who's speaking, please?"

"This is Bruce King at Jentech."

"Yes, Mr. King. How can I help you?"

He had worked on a little job for Jentech two years earlier.

"We've had a break-in and sabotage."

A short silence followed.

"I'm sorry to hear that."

"Someone managed to delete important files from our mainframe, and from the personal computers of a number of our employees."

"A physical break-in, you mean?"

"Yes. There's no evidence of one, however. No er, broken windows or such. Nothing is broken. But it looks like the computer drives have been damaged deliberately. We're not certain how yet. What we are certain of is that a number of documents have been taken from desks and filing cabinets. In concert with the damage to the computers we're quite certain it's sabotage."

Once there, it did not take a genius to figure out what had happened.

"So this product... who would want it not to come out?"

"Well, our major competitors, I suppose."

"Who are?"

"Probably SpecterWare."

"Do you have any employees here who used to work for them?"

Not only did they have one, but also he'd only started the previous week. A check with the logbook kept by the guard showed he had been the last to leave the previous night.

"But how could he have gained entry? The doors were locked," King protested.

"Perhaps he had a spare key?"

"No. Impossible. It's an electronic lock, and according to the records no one passed through the corridor door except the guard on his hourly rounds."

"I'd like to speak to the guard on duty."

"He's at home, of course. He won't be in until four."

"Do you have his address?"

***

An hour later Collin emerged from the guard's flat, smiling to himself.

"I love it when things are this easy," he said to himself.

Solving the puzzle this quickly would make him look very good to Jentech, which would eagerly recommend him to other companies in need. Business was getting better.

The guard hadn't wanted to tell him what had happened, of course. But the threat of being arrested won out over his fear of being fired. It wasn't like it was that good a job anyway.

Peter Cross had worked late, and a gorgeous blonde, supposedly his wife, had come on to the guard, thrown herself at him, and distracted him, keeping him away from the lobby. Then Cross had taken his key card and, either alone or with someone else he had let in, had done what had been done.

So Collin knew how they'd done it. But he still had no absolute proof. He needed to get the blonde or her boyfriend - supposing it really was her boyfriend, which he doubted - to tell him who was behind them. Then Jentech would be able to sue SpecterWare. With a little luck (which he would make for himself if necessary) word of this would leak out. The tabloids would love it, especially if the blonde was as attractive as the guard claimed, and the name of his "firm" would be prominently mentioned as having quickly solved the case.

This Peter Cross fellow was at work at Jentech, being watched discreetly. He would have a word with him and see what could be gained. He drove back to Jentech and had King set aside an office for his use, then had Peter Cross summoned.

***

Peter was more than slightly nervous when he was asked to come to the office of his supervisor, Mark Chambers. There he was introduced to a very large man named Butler, who Chambers identified as their security supervisor. This immediately caused his anxiety to rise, despite Butler's reassuring smile.

"Speak to Mr. Butler, Peter, and... tell him whatever it is

he wants to know," Chambers said.

"Of course, Mark," he said, trying to appear unconcerned.

Chambers left, closing the door, and Butler motioned Peter to sit, then stared at him for a long minute.

"What er, is this about?" Peter asked, unable to bear the silence.

"I'm investigating a break-in at Jentech the other day," Butler said.

"Oh. Er, was anything stolen?"

"We're not sure, but there was some damage done to computers."

"Vandals," Peter said with a poor attempt at a smile.

"Perhaps."

"Well, er, what else could it be? If none of the computers were stolen..."

"We don't know information wasn't stolen. We certainly know information was destroyed."

"Really?"

"Yes." Butler turned and smiled at him. "Do you happen to know a lovely young woman with blonde hair, Peter?"

"Well, er, I know a few blonde women."

"This one was rather unforgettable. I'm told she had an insatiable sexual appetite, as if she couldn't get enough, as if she were a starving woman finally given food. You know what I mean? Like a woman who hadn't been ridden properly in all her life and finally had a good one between her legs."

Peter flushed unhappily.

"The man I talked to described her as the biggest whore he'd ever met, almost a nymphomaniac. He said she could hardly stop coming once he got his hands on her. Sound like anyone you know?"

"I don't think so," Peter replied sullenly.

"She had short hair, very soft hair. The man I spoke to described how he couldn't stop running his fingers through her hair as she worked her lips up and down on his cock. She took the whole thing down her throat. Can you imagine that? She must really love cock." He laughed, shaking his head. "Maybe when I find this little slut I'll give her a little of it myself, just to show her how a real man does it."

"I'm not feeling very well. Perhaps if we could do this another day..."

"Oh we won't take long. Don't worry. I'm sure we can get you something to drink that will make you feel better."

There was silence in the room for a moment, and Butler took a stick of chewing gum out of his pocket, popping it into his mouth, and offered one to Peter, who declined.

"Anyway," Butler said around the gum, "we figure this little tart distracted the guard, you see, bending over and shoving it in his face like that, and while she was grunting like a bitch in heat, someone sneaked in somehow and got at the computers. They used his key card to get through the doors, too."

He nodded thoughtfully, switching the gum to the other side of his mouth.

"Of course, the front door was locked, so whoever did it was probably in the building already, waiting for this cheap slag to bend herself across the desk and spread her legs before snatching it and going upstairs."

Peter scowled and looked out of the window.

"There was only one person in the building at the time, Mr. Cross. Guess who that was."

"I'm sure I could not imagine," Peter retorted.

"Why it was you, my friend." Butler grinned knowingly.

"Are you accusing me of destroying these computers?" Peter demanded, feigning outrage.

"Not destroyed, Pete. Likely someone just ran a magnet across them."

"I would never do something like that!"

"By coincidence, this blonde slut identified herself as your wife."

"I'm not married."

Butler laughed. "No, of course you're not. And if the description of this big titted blonde is right I can hardly see her marrying some piddling little technician with his nose buried in a computer manual. But it is odd she said she was your wife."

"Perhaps they knew I was the only one in the building."

"True. That's a possibility. But the guard called up and you talked to her."

"Oh that," Peter said, forcing a laugh.

"That." Butler nodded.

"The guard did call up. I thought he was drunk, saying my wife was there, so I told him to put her on. Some woman came on and raved about something or other. Didn't even answer my questions about who she was, and then hung up."

"Do tell?" Butler sneered in a disbelieving tone.

"Yes, well, I just went back to my work, I thought the guard was having a joke on me."

"Didn't you try and call security, find out what was happening?"

"I don't have the number for the security desk."

"You could have gone downstairs."

"Wasn't my business? Anyway, I was working."

"I suppose that's true. But you know, when this sluttish little tart was done sucking off the guard, done fucking him and milking him of every drop of semen she could, and the guard finally returned to his post, he found the building empty. You'd apparently left some time earlier."

"Yes," Peter nodded vigorously. "In fact, I did go downstairs, and planned to ask the guard what on Earth that conversation had been about, but he was nowhere around. I waited for several minutes, then finally just left."

'Ahhh." Butler appeared to consider the explanation. "So you didn't put this woman up to it, hmm?"

"Me?"

"You didn't find some whore and pay her to distract the guard?"

"How dare you..."

"Oh shut it," Butler said. "We know it was you. We know you found some slut to distract that guard. I bet you even got your jollies looking in at them through the window. Did it give you a hard-on, Peter, to see this hot blonde being royally fucked? Or did it make you jealous that he was doing so much better a job of it than you could have?"

Peter stood up. "I refuse to be insulted like this any further!"

"Sit down or I'll put you down."

"You wouldn't dare touch me!" Peter challenged.

"Why not?"

"Because... because I shall call the police."

Butler guffawed, slapping the desk with a hand so large it echoed like a gunshot.

"You won't do that, Pete. If you did the whole world would know what a simpering little wretch you are. They'd find out all about you pimping girls to security guards, and sabotaging computers. What a scandal that would be. The tabloids would love pictures of the girl and you, and you'd never find another job again."

"This is all nonsense. I've done nothing!"

"I don't believe you."

***

Collin worked on the man for more than an hour. Peter Cross was a terrible liar. Everything he said was so obviously, patently untrue, said in a squirming, shifty-eyed manner, which would have made even the truth sound like a lie. Yet short of beating the piss out of him Collin was at a loss to get him to change his story. He decided to back off, and instead watch him leave. He locked him in the office and gave instructions for him to be fired after a ten-minute period, and sent packing

That was enough time for him to get downstairs, bring his car around, and wait near Cross's car to see where it led. He was betting Cross was too dumb to lay low, that he would head straight for whoever had put him up to this sabotage, and perhaps to a hot blonde with big breasts too.

He sat in his car, slumped back, playing a portable Nintendo game while he waited for Cross to leave. He was so engrossed in the game he almost missed him, and had to drop it on the floor and scramble to start the car when Cross' Ford turned onto the street ahead of him.

As was the usual case his subject hadn't a clue anyone might be following him and made no effort to check. Collin had no difficulty keeping pace as the man drove only a short distance across the city to SpecterWare. He was even close enough, when he stopped, to get out his camera and take pictures of the man hurrying in through the door.

Jentech would love such pictures, he thought happily, and they'd look good to a jury, as well.

He watched employees streaming out of the building, and settled down to wait.

The wait was much longer than he had expected, however, and he was replacing the worn out batteries in his machine when he caught movement at a small side-door, which led to the building's parking lot. It was dark, but he had a vision enhancing nightscope, which he had fortuitously removed from the boot of his car a half-hour earlier. Thus he was able to see, to his considerable astonishment, Peter Cross coming out of the door, naked, collared, and leashed, and crawling across the parking lot at the heels of a tall blonde woman with a look of profound arrogance on her face.

"I'll be damned!" he whispered aloud in amazement.

He was too shocked to even think about his camera, which, in any case, was loaded with the wrong kind of film for night work. He watched in fascination as the blonde opened the boot of his car and Cross climbed inside. She then tossed the leash in after him and slammed the boot closed before going around to the driver's door and getting in.

He started sniggering to himself, and then guffawed delightedly as the car started up and its lights came on. He had been looking for who gave orders and he had certainly found her. More, he was beginning to suspect a connection between this tall, beautiful blonde who was obviously involved in industrial espionage with Jentech, and the tall, beautiful blonde involved in industrial espionage at Ecom.

Which in turn led him to suspect exactly why Jeffrey Fitzwilliams was being less than forthcoming about how the information had been taken in the first place. He imagined Fitzwilliams crawling along on a leash and snickered to himself as he started his car, then turned to follow the blonde.

They drove south, crossed the river, and stopped before a small townhouse. The street was quite dark; the hedges around the small front gardens helped conceal the sight of Peter Cross crawling nude up the pavement and then into the house. They would also conceal himself, he decided.

He walked casually along the pavement, up the short path, slid aside at the door, and then, as natural as if he were at his own home, walked across to the windows, only to find the blinds tightly drawn. He made a face, then walked back to the street and continued around to the rear of the building. He crossed the yards of several other homes before reaching the proper yard, then crouched low, studying the rear door and windows.

It was a warm night, yet all the blinds were tightly drawn, all the windows closed shut. He pondered this, and felt a small stirring of sexual interest as he imagined the lewd goings on inside which were the probably cause.

He removed a sharp folding knife from his pocket and then moved slowly towards a low basement window, laying on his belly before it and looking around carefully to see if he had been observed. He studied the screen over the window and then used the knife to carefully cut along the edge, easing the screen up to give him access to the window.

The window was quite simple, made up of one immovable pane of glass set in an immovable frame, and an offset window which slid horizontally back. The building was old, and the wood around the windows was warped and slightly rotting. He was able to carefully dig away at the wood where he estimated a locking device would be placed, and after some minutes was rewarded by exposing a small steel hook. He smiled, placed the knife blade beneath it, and slowly lifted it up. He then eased the window slightly open with the blade.

He had heard soft mumbles while working, and now those voices became clear.

"...Miserable slut," he heard a woman say. "Do you think I intend to let you go without punishment for such stupidity?"

"I'm sorry mistress," he heard a man's low, whiny voice say.

He rolled his eyes, then slid the knife blade forward, enough to touch the edge of the curtain blocking his view, and ease it gently aside, just enough to expose a crack to place his eye to.

The basement was brightly lit, and his jaw dropped at the scene exposed before him. Peter Cross was hanging upside down, nude, his ankles spread wide apart. The blonde, as naked as him, and as spectacularly built as the guard had described, stood before him holding what looked like an altar candle in her hands. As he watched she tipped it and hot wax dribbled down over Cross's erection, producing a howl of pain.

Collin watched, fascinated, as the blonde let wax dribble all over the man's groin, over his erection, his testicles, his thighs and buttocks, then spread the cheeks of the latter and somehow managed to force the thick candle down into his rectum. It fitted tightly, and stood upright, still alight, still burning, tilting from side to side as his body moved to tip wax down onto his groin.

"Jesus, Mary and Joseph!" Collin whispered, growing erect himself.

He considered a number of things as he observed the lewd goings on. Principally, he wished he had a camera, preferably a video camera. This was something the fellows at the pub would never believe.

And then a powerful knee jammed into the small of his back, and as he cried out in pain a hand yanked his wrist around behind him, snapping a handcuff over it. He was off balance and taken by surprise. He jerked his head up, only to hit it against the top of the window frame. His other wrist was pulled behind, locked to the first, and then a dark, shadowed hand yanked the window fully open and shoved him forward through it.

He yelled in confusion and pain as he plummeted to the floor. He managed to twist his body slightly, so that he landed on his shoulder rather than his head, but cried out in pain at the impact.

Kathleen appeared overhead, glaring down at him, and then reached past him to the window, she nodded at someone there, then closed the window tightly and returned her attention to him.

"Well, well, a little peeping tom," she said scornfully.

"Hurts, does it? Too bad. Next time you'll learn not to peep in people's windows." She rolled him onto his stomach, ignoring his cry of pain, and yanked his wallet out of his back pocket, then opened it and wandered back to a chair, sitting leisurely and opening it. He rolled back onto his back, then, hissing in pain, sat up, just as another woman came down the stairs. This was the black girl Fitzwilliams had described, big, powerful, huge shoulders, grim faced, long hair. Yes, it was her, and he cursed himself for having forgotten all about her.

"His name appears to be Collin Butler," Kathleen said, leafing through his papers and cards.

"Should I call the police?"

The blonde hesitated, then her eyes narrowed and she looked back at him.

"It says here he's a private detective."

The black woman gave a bark of laughter, and then almost immediately frowned herself.

She crossed the floor and searched him further, pulling out his small notebook. He wrote very little, and what he did write was abrupt and in bad penmanship, but the woman's eyes jerked up as she saw something, then she held the book out to Kathleen.

"Jentech," she read. "Meeting at 11:a.m."

They both turned their eyes to him.

"What were you doing at Jentech?" she asked.

"Undo my hands!" he demanded, pain and anger making his voice harsh.

"Kathleen, look."

The black woman had found something else of interest in the notebook.

"You met with Fitzwilliams? I know a Fitzwilliams," she said, looking at him.

"I'll just bet you do, darling," he said, smirking cynically.

"What did you do to him anyway?"

"You may find out if you don't tell us what you were doing peeping into our window," Kathleen warned.

"I'm not one of your simpering little pansies."

She smiled thinly and waved nonchalantly.

Yvette moved forward and as Collin tried to stand put a foot against the centre of his chest and flung him backwards. She dropped quickly to her knees, one knee slamming into his groin so that his eyes bulged and his curse became a croak. Then she efficiently undid his belt and trousers, yanking the latter down, along with his shorts. She untied his shoes and pulled them off, then slid the entire lot off, leaving him nude below the waist. She rolled him onto his belly, then picked up his own knife, using it to slash open his shirt and peel it off.

Collin cursed her, but with his hands cuffed he had little chance to fight back. When she was done she rose, gripping his chained wrists and lifting up hard, forcing him to his feet, then forward, arms high, body bent painfully forward. She led him to a position not far from where Peter Cross hung, then reached above for a hook attached to another chain. She fitted the hook under the link of his cuffs, and Kathleen pulled on another crank to raise the chain higher.

"Christ!"

Kathleen smiled.

"Big, strong man," she taunted. "But there isn't anything you can do to resist, now is there?"

"As soon as I get out of this..."

"But you won't unless I wish it. Now, tell me what you know."

"Get stuffed you fucking weirdoes!"

She slapped his face hard, and he tried to spit at her.

She slapped his face again, then, using both hands, began to slap him first from the right, then the left, each time throwing his head violently aside.

He groaned dazedly when she stopped, and she reached for his hair, gripping it and using it to lift his head. "Tell me what you know."

She stepped on his bare toes, grinding the sole of her shoe down and he clenched his teeth and said nothing. She shifted her foot and pressed the heel down just above his toes. He screamed and cursed explosively.

"Big strong man," she sneered, "I think I'll make you my next lap dog. Would you like that? Do you think you'll be capable of licking my shoes with the proper humility?"

She pressed her sex to his face.

"Show me what else you can do with that tongue, pretty boy," she demanded.

He closed his jaw tightly, and she laughed, grinding her sex against his closed lips.

"You think you're tough, big man?" she sneered. "But it's all just pride. And we know what to do about male pride, don't we, Yvette?"

Yvette handed her a long dildo attached to a set of straps and Kathleen released Collin's hair to step into the straps and draw them up her body then fastened the buckles tightly so that the dildo sprang forward from her groin.

"Care to reconsider, pretty boy?" she taunted.

Yvette pulled Collin's head up so that he must stare at the thick dildo, and kissed the side of his face gently.

"Have you ever been sodomised, sweet boy?" she purred. "You're going to like this very much."

Collin cursed them both furiously, thrashing against the cuffs as Kathleen moved behind. He tried to kick back at her like a mule, and Yvette quickly seized his ankles, then strapped them to a spread bar which was locked down to the floor. This increased the pressure on his shoulders as his arms were raised even higher behind him, but he continued to curse and struggle.

"Male pride," Kathleen said softly stroking his buttocks and reaching between his legs to fondle his groin.

Then she pressed the rounded head of the dildo against his anus and pushed forward. His thrashing grew more intense and his curses and threats louder. Yvette yanked on his hair hard, and with his mouth wide, shoved a penis gag into it, giggling at him as he glowered savagely at her.

"You suck on that, pretty boy," she teased, strapping it behind his head.

Kathleen was not gentle, thrusting strongly against him, forcing the thick dildo deeper and deeper into his rectum as he grunted and cursed through the gag.

"What a choice bit of arse," she said, slapping at his bottom as she lunged forward.

She rammed the dildo fully inside him and ground her hips against his buttocks in a slow, taunting circular motion. Her hands caressed his body, reaching beneath to pinch and tug and twist at his nipples. Then she began to stroke in and out, using raw force to tear her way through the clutches of his reluctant sphincter muscle.

"Don't be so upset," she said sweetly. "Before long you'll learn to love it. You'll beg for me to take you."

She pumped faster, harder, using long, full strokes, her hips slapping against his buttocks. Yvette, meanwhile, knelt to his side, reached up, and snapped two strong alligator clips onto his nipples. Each dangled a three-inch long chain, from which hung a heavy weight. She reached between his legs then, snapping another such clip against his soft, fleshy penis, the sharp little jaws biting in just behind the head. He gave a violent lurch and his muffled curses grew louder.

She teased the head of his cock with another, then let it snap onto the soft skin of his scrotum. Another clip was then fastened directly against the tip of his cock, and she let it snap shut, releasing the weight so it would dangle freely.

Kathleen laughed and stopped her pumping motion, then unbuckled the straps, turning them inside out and buckling them around Collin so that the dildo remained buried inside him.

"We'll give you a little time to think about things, big man," she purred.

CHAPTER TWELVE

"How much do you think Jentech knows about us?" Yvette asked in the upstairs room.

"I don't know. It's not a good sign that he came right to us, though."

"What should we do?"

"Keep him here and find out what he knows."

"What about Fitzwilliams?"

Kathleen smiled. "I think we can take care of Fitzwilliams."

"But..."

"Yvette, the stock has almost doubled since I bought it. It's starting to create interest in all the right places. Once Charles lets out that information on our new products we can expect the present stock price to double, at least. From there, momentum might carry us anywhere. But we need to have those products advanced enough to show to the analysts. We're just not ready. We need another few months."

"So what do we do?"

"You go and get Fitzwilliams. I'll take this one's keys and go to his office and house to see what he might have written down. If he hasn't told Jentech about us then we've nothing to fear."

"We can't keep him for months."

"We could, but we might not need to, if we can train him

as you did Fitzwilliams."

"Fitzwilliams is obviously looking for us."

"Yes, but he hasn't told him why, nor has he told anyone else, nor even warned his own company about our er, competition. We can handle big man, don't worry."

She returned to the cellar, and her eyes moved back and forth between Peter and Collin Butler. She removed Butler's gag, and he coughed and spat.

"See how considerate I can be?" she said sweetly.

"Bitch," he spat angrily at her.

She sighed dramatically. "I'm going over to your flat and see what I can turn up. You'd do well to reconsider this obstinate approach. It will really get you nowhere."

"I'll have you locked up! I'll have you..."

She slapped his face and then walked up the stairs, slamming the door behind her. She did not close it, however, merely let it hit the frame and come open again, then sat on the top stair to listen and see what she could discover.

At first there was only the occasional grunt and gasp, and she remembered Peter's candle was still lit. She smiled, but had little fear. The candle was thick as a strong man's wrist, and would take hours to burn down to him.

"Is this what you get off on?" she heard Butler snarl.

Peter didn't answer.

"This is why you did it, isn't it? Because your bloody mistress told you to!"

"Yes," Peter panted.

"You fucking pansy! Does she spank you if you don't go on your pee-potty right?"

"You'll find out," Peter replied solemnly.

"You simpering little bastard!"

"She'll punish you if you keep swearing," Peter said.

"Let the bitch try! When I get out of here I'll have her guts for garters!"

Peter laughed weakly. "Going to set the police on her?" he asked his voice distorted by his pain and discomfort. "Going to tell the police how she stuck you up the arse with a dildo?"

"I wouldn't talk!"

"I won't talk."

There was silence for a bit.

"I don't need the police to teach that slut a lesson. I know people. I know a French pimp who could use a new girl for his stable. And he knows how to handle highly strung bitches."

Peter laughed weakly. "And Kathleen knows how to handle highly strung bastards like you," he said defensively.

Collin cursed him.

"She can't hold me forever. I'll get out of these, and then look out!"

***

This sounded quite promising to Kathleen. There was nothing in Butler's words about rescue, nothing to suggest that he would be freed because someone knew where he was and what he was doing, no hint that soon the police or unknown partners would come around to ask harsh questions.

She got up, closed the door softly, bolted it, and then went for her car. It was a short trip to the address in his wallet, a seedy looking building in Northeast London.

Kathleen looked around the bedroom in distaste. It was just the kind of a room a rutting, macho man would live in, she thought. A pair of tables, each of which contained numerous pornographic magazines and books, as well as condoms in multiple colours, lubricant and, she smirked, pink furred handcuffs, framed the big waterbed in the corner.

There was a cheap erotic painting on one wall which had likely come from a department store, and a framed blown-up colour picture of one of the page three girls, wearing the remnants of a torn white thong and little else. In one drawer was a collection of Polaroid photos of naked women, apparently souvenirs of this or that brief encounter. There was also one picture of a man's groin, showing a long, thick, bulging erection. After a moment she decided it was likely his. Did he show it to sluts at the discos to pick them up, she wondered.

He certainly was thick, however.

His suits were cheap, his shoes worse. The man had no style at all. He was in fact a fashion nightmare, a mish-mash of garish and totally unsuitable clothing.

In the front room she found a bundle of papers on a cheap table, but nothing mentioning her or SpecterWare. There was a phone book with the names of numerous technology companies in them, and names, apparently contacts, within these companies. From this she decided he likely worked for any number of companies within the industry, and so had only been called by Jentech recently. How much, she wondered had he told them? Anything? And what had he done with Peter?

Big, stupid, crude ignorant macho man! She had never intended to get involved in the kind of lawbreaking which might see the police looking for her one day. But she was not about to let him get in the way of her accumulating the wealth she had always dreamed of. If she had to keep him in chains for three months that was exactly what she would do. And when she was done with him he would be no more eager than Fitzwilliams to go to the authorities.

***

Collin groaned at the punishment his shoulders were taking. His arms felt ready to rip free. His back ached, and he was getting dazed from having his head hanging down for so long. The clips biting into his nipples, cock and scrotum were sharp little daggers of pain, and any movement set the weights to swinging and swaying, pulling down more sharply.

He found his current situation almost unbelievable, and his outrage fought with humiliation and disbelief. No one had ever succeeded in treating him like this. No one had ever even tried. He couldn't imagine his worst enemy daring to try. Then again, all his enemies were men.

He imagined himself getting free, imagined himself capturing the blonde bitch, raping her, sodomising her, stringing her up and whipping her again and again. He imagined handing her over, drugged and dazed, to the most brutal pimp he knew, to be put on the streets. Ten, twenty men a day would use her, drunken pigs that would rut like animals. He'd show her all right. He'd show them both!

He groaned helplessly, hardly aware of the time now, or of how long he had been bound. He looked up at the sound of feet on the stairs, and his eyes saw the black girl step gracefully over a low bench and approach him, smiling. He glowered at her bitterly and let his head hang once more.

***

Yvette examined the panting, sweating man carefully. There were time limits beyond which it was best not to leave a slave bound in particular positions. Exceeding those limits risked permanent damage. Yet this man was unlike any others she had previously held bound. It wasn't merely that he was an unwilling "guest", but that he obviously had both great strength and the will to use it if she gave him any opportunity. Changing his position without doing so might be a challenge.

Of course, modern technology was always a great help in overcoming challenges.

She lowered the chain holding his wrists aloft. This permitted him to sink to his knees on the floor, where his eyes continued to glare murderously at her.

"You should be grateful," she said lightly.

He did not, however, look at all grateful.

She removed the hook, allowing him to drop his arms. He shuddered in relief, rolling his powerful shoulders, and she smiled down at him.

"You must realise," she said, "that further rudeness will only result in more discomfort."

She kicked lightly at the weight dangling from his scrotum and watched it swing back and forth.

'Fucking Christ!" he cried in agony.

"You're going to be a challenge," she said, smiling. "I like challenges."

First, of course, she must weaken him in both mind and body. Depriving him of food, water and sleep would help there, and keeping him in positions of physical discomfort would accentuate his helplessness.

"Stand up," she said.

He continued to glower murderously at her, and she gripped a fistful of hair and tugged up until, snarling and writhing, he managed to rise to his feet before her. Even with his legs apart, held in place by the spreader bar, he was taller than her, and she let her hands move thoughtfully over his body as she studied him. He did not have the kind of perfectly defined muscles that her other slaves did, the ones she had ordered to work out in order to achieve the body she liked. Instead he was simply big all over, with a thick, hairy chest and powerful arms and shoulders. His stomach was smooth, flat, and had muscles behind it, but without the washboard appearance she liked.

His groin was hairy, too hairy. She fondled his cock speculatively. It was quite big and thick, even flaccid, and would look bigger still once his pubic hair was trimmed back.

"Perhaps you would like a little bath?" she said brightly.

"Fuck off," he gasped.

She smiled, kneeing him in the groin almost absently. As he gasped and choked and moaned she turned and fetched the hose, then turned it on and wetted him down. The water soaked him, raining down to pool on the floor around him. The pool grew no more than a few feet in width and length, however, for there was a small drain at one end of it.

"Mistress," Peter groaned.

"I'll see to you later, Peter," she said, her eyes remaining on Butler.

She soaked him, then fetched over a pair of scissors. Cutting off his pubic hair would serve to humiliate him more, and make him feel more vulnerable. She cut his dark hair down short, then spread soap over his groin.

"Don't touch me," he said through gritted teeth.

"Shhh! Don't be a silly little boy," she replied easily.

She began to shave quickly, using confident strokes, gripping his cock and tugging it from one side to the other, ignoring his humiliated curses as she handled him. She removed the clips from his cock and scrotum, and he cursed in pain. She ignored him, pulling his flaccid cock out, stretching it, and then running the razor along it from all sides. It did not surprise her when he began to thicken and harden. The pain from the newly released clips would now be turning to an enormous sense of relief, and his cock would be sensitive and eager for pleasurable sensations.

"Are you excited about being shaved?" she asked in a taunting voice.

She fondled him further, massaging his testicles, stroking his cock, and he continued to harden.

"I can see you are. You're an eager little thing, aren't you?"

He was growing impressively thick, and she pumped him

with her hand as he looked away, teeth clenched.

"If you're good, perhaps I'll fuck you later," she said.

With his cock hard, the skin taut, it was easier to shave, and she continued to do so. When she was done she pushed him backwards, forcing him down onto his back on the floor then attached a chain to the centre of the spreader bar and lifted his ankles up and back. She then shaved his bottom and inner thighs while he continued to curse weakly.

With that done she decided to raise the spreader higher, letting him dangle upside down like Peter was.

"Well, big man, what are we to do with you? You're getting in the way of some very important work, you know. If you'd only co-operate we could carry on and you might even find yourself rewarded.

"F-fuck you!" he snarled angrily.

"Now that isn't nice," she responded in a wounded tone.

"When I get my hands on you you'll find out just how not nice I can be!"

"But I'm the one who has her hands on you," she purred, pumping her fist up and down the length of his still hard cock.

"Why don't you put your lips around it so I can shove it down your throat?" he snarled as a challenge.

"Because you're not being a good boy," she said.

Yvette moved back and picked up the hose, then moved to the wall and turned the water pressure up. She turned off the hot water and moved back to where Collin hung. She smiled, let the water play over his cursing body, rinsing off the soap from his groan, then pulled the dildo out of his rectum and shoved the hose in.

He howled and snarled, twisting and thrashing on the end of the chain, and she laughed, pulling the hose back. He was no longer erect.

"That seems to have cooled you off some."

"Fucking bitch!"

She smiled and sprayed him again, watching in amusement as it trickled down across down his body and fell over his face.

"You'll have to learn better manners, big man," she said.

He cursed her again, predictably, she thought. He really didn't have a very good vocabulary of threats.

She put the hose away and picked up Kathleen's stun gun, then placed the boxy device against his still soaking wet penis and fired it. He let out a squawk, his body jerking violently, then went limp, his jaw slack.

She smiled and watched him hang there a bit then turned and pulled the candle out of Peter's bottom, blew it out, and set it aside. She lowered him to the floor, and let him recover somewhat, before ordering him upstairs to take a bath.

She turned back to Collin Butler, who was only then beginning to moan dazedly. She moved behind him. His wrist restraints were clipped together at the small of his back. She unclipped them, attaching first one, then the other to separate chains which she then raised up and apart. This raised his torso upwards so that he hung almost horizontally, arms and legs up and apart.

The weights were still dangling from his nipples. She waited until he had regained his senses before re-attaching the weights to his scrotum and cock. Then, as he howled, she climbed onto his back and straddled him. He grunted in pain at the addition of more than a hundred and sixty pounds of muscular female to the pressure pulling on his arms and legs, but did not speak. She swung her legs briefly, then leaned forward, pulling his hair to force his head up and back, and speaking cordially into his ear.

"Do you like boys, big man?" she asked. "I can give Peter to you, you know? I can let you do anything you want to him, as often as you want. He's a lovely little thing, isn't he?"

"Fuck off," he said though clenched teeth. "I'm not a ponce! I'll show you as much as soon as I get out of here. I'll fuck you so hard you won't close your legs for a month!"

"Promises, promises," she said, smiling.

She swung her legs over his side and stepped off, then moved around between his legs. She picked up the strap-on dildo from the floor and strapped it to her loins, then thrust it into him and began to slowly pump the big dildo in and out.

"Admit you like it," she taunted. "You men are always afraid of admitting it because you think it makes you queer."

He glared grimly at the floor and said nothing, and she giggled, pumping harder, sliding her hands up and down his body, and then going beneath him to massage his cock. She released the clips on his cock and scrotum and they dropped to the floor, but she knew, despite the resulting curses, that the pain of returning blood flow would once again flood him with relief. And that the wonderful sensation of cooling pleasure would do lovely things to his cock. She continued to pump, thrusting harder now, massaging his cock, stroking his buttocks, and feeling him harden in her fingers.

"That's it, slut. Get hard for Yvette. Show her how much you like it."

She fingered and massaged his nipples, leaning across his body now to lick and chew on the nape of his neck. "Pretty boy," she whispered, her behind rising and falling as she rode him. She unclipped the weights and let them fall too, and after another minute of cursing, when the relief flooded in him, and despite his best efforts, he soon came, spurting his white excitement onto the floor below him as the black woman thrust deep into his rectum.

She laughed tauntingly at him, unstrapped the dildo, and reversed the straps, and fastened it once again around his hips. She then picked up one of the weights she had dropped. She moved around in front of him, and yanked back hard on his hair. Quick as a viper she jammed the alligator clip forward into his mouth, got the open jaws around his tongue, and dropped it.

His curses turned to a snarl of outrage and pain, and she quickly snapped the second weight onto the first one, to force his tongue out further and prevent him from using his teeth to free it. She laughed in his face at his discomfort and pain, then fetched the other clips and weights. Soon weights were dangling from his nipples once more, as well as from his scrotum and penis.

"We want that tongue of yours to get more exercise," she told him. "But not for talking. "Learn to push it out far from your big mouth and you'll begin to be worth something around here."

She placed a strap around his forehead, then pulled it up and back, running the strap into a chain and attaching that to the base of the dildo buried in his rectum. Then, with his head held in position, she kissed him delicately on the bridge of his nose, turned, and left.

She got upstairs just as Kathleen came through the door, and they nodded to each other.

"I didn't find much at his piss-pot little office," she said. "There was a computer but I wiped it. There was nothing with our names on it. I didn't find anything at his house flat either.

"I did see an entry in a ledger that he'd been hired by our friend Jeffrey, however. Jeffrey didn't tell him much, just that these two evil women had stolen some information from him.... We'll have to make him pay for that 'Evil'"

"Who? Jeffrey or big man?"

"Why not both?" she questioned lightly.

'Works for me."

"Where is he now?"

"Downstairs, hanging by his wrists and ankles."

"And dear Peter?" she enquired with a hint of concern in her voice.

"Sent him upstairs to wash off the wax."

Kathleen nodded.

"Think we're getting into things too deeply?"

"We're in too deep to back out now."

"But this guy is no Jeffrey. He's going to be harder to break."

"We don't have to break him. We can just keep him here for a while."

"For two or three months?"

"If necessary. What would you rather? Let him go and hope he doesn't put us in the same positions?"

"Not hardly."

"Then we've little choice. You should be off to work soon."

Yvette nodded. "Going to seem boring after big man. You should see that cock of his. I shaved it and when it's erect it's a monster."

"You shaved it? Interesting idea."

"Unlike you, I like to wrap my lips around a nice fat cock now and then," Yvette said with a grin. "Getting rid of the hair makes it seem so much... smoother."

Kathleen rolled her eyes. "Slut."

"Whore." Yvette grinned. "I didn't fuck him. I figured to save that for a reward, but he has a beautiful cock, so I'm not sure if he's the one who'll get the reward or me."

"Well, I'll go down and see him."

"I only just hung him up. Give him half an hour or so."

Kathleen nodded and went upstairs. She stripped and put on a simple cotton thong and midriff baring tank top, then went to see Peter.

He was just drying off after his shower, and beamed happily at her.

"Peter," she said brightly. "You look positively naked."

Peter looked confused and she gave a mental sigh. Peter was a sweet boy but rather helpless.

"No restraints? No shackles?"

"I'm sorry mistress."

Too broken this one. Too easy.

"You had better send your CV around again. Leave out your recent stay with Jentech, of course."

"Yes mistress."

Peter walked across the hall to the spare room, where her computer was. He pushed away the padded chair she used and slid over the hard wooden chair she had set out for him. There was a ten-inch wooden penis glued in its centre on its base, and he squatted over it, then slowly lowered himself down, becoming erect as he did so. She watched him adjust himself carefully, wincing a little then setting to work at the computer.

She found herself smiling. Peter really was such a pet - literally.

She went back downstairs and looked into the refrigerator, brooding slightly. Her plan was really going so well before this happened. It was all due to simple bad luck, to Jentech having that new product just about ready to go at the worst possible time. Without any real word of what kind of new products SpecterWare was bringing out the sudden blow that new product would have given them would have shaken the confidence of all the new shareholders and they'd have bolted en masse, dropping the stock price into the toilet.

Bad luck was not going to screw her out of her wealth. Nothing was. She was going to have a big house, and servants and all the respect that went with it.

She bent and picked out one of the large cucumbers, smiling. Yvette insisted on buying them, and had a delightful time eating them in front of her, teasing her. Of course, when they were in the mood, or had drunk a bit much, they made other uses of the thick green vegetables.

She thought of Collin Butler, then for some reason thought of Devon Winchester. The smile left her face and a scowl replaced it. Winchester had been principal of students at Northrup College, a pale, whey faced little man with no chin. A more arrogant bastard she'd never met. She'd been eighteen, and in her second year when she'd been called into his office. A look of contempt had been on his face from the moment she'd set foot inside.

"Miss Hunter, I presume," he'd said, in a thin, arrogant voice dripping with upper class condescension.

"Yes, sir," she'd responded.

He'd examined her academic record, he said, and found it highly puzzling.

"We take special care to examine our, er, scholarship students backgrounds," he said, saying the word as if it stood in substitution of "welfare" or "criminal". But somehow or other, we missed you last year. In any case, now that you've come to our attention..."

"Sir?"

He frowned at her impertinence in speaking. "Your off campus activities, Miss Hunter," he said in disgust. "Or had you been under the illusion we would not discover them?"

"I'm not certain what you are referring to."

"Are you not? Perhaps you think working in a... a place like the... the..." He picked up a piece of paper in irritation, read it, and looked up at her once again. "The Black Tail Lounge," he said caustically. "Is a fitting use of your..." He looked her up and down contemptuously. "Talents."

He continued, "But it makes Northrup look quite bad to have our female students prostituting their bodies in a cheap bar!"

"I'm not prostituting myself!" she said, shocked.

He gave her a withering look. "I am told you wear a G-string, and a tailored tuxedo coat with neither a top nor trousers."

"Well, but it mostly covers everything," she said defensively.

He sat behind an enormous chair and stared at her for a long moment.

"It's perfectly legal! And there's no, no prostitution involved!' she exclaimed. "How dare you even think it like that!"

"Why do you work there?"

"Because I need the money!" she responded sarcastically.

"Why do you have to work there? There?"

"It pays well," she said resentfully.

"And why does it pay so well?" he asked as if speaking to an ignorant child.

She was silent.

"Because showing off your nearly naked body draws large tips from the clientele, of course. Don't try to bandy words with me, girl. You haven't the wit."

"I do well in school and..."

"Yes, let's examine that," he said, leaning forward. "I examined your academic record. It's odd, but up until you turned sixteen you were a slightly sub-average student. Suddenly your marks began to rise. The only subjects which you continued to fare poorly in were, oddly enough, those where the instructor was female."

He looked up at her. "Interesting that you chose computer engineering, where almost all the instructors are male."

"I-I'm not sure what you're suggesting, sir?" she said, white-faced.

"What I'm suggesting is that if I were to give you an examination based on the work you did so very well in last year I suspect you would fare quite poorly. Because I suspect you're getting your marks by spreading your legs for your professors."

She gaped at him, both outraged by his contemptuous attitude, and frightened because he was right.

"Don't gape at me, you slut. Do you think I haven't seen your like before? You gutter crawling sluts from the slums trying to sleep your way into success?"

"I-I haven't, I mean, I wouldn't..."

He stood up and raised his hand, holding a sheet of paper.

"This is an expulsion order. It has your name on it."

She stared at him in shock.

"Of course, it's purely up to me as to whether I sign it or not."

The corners of his lips curled upwards in a lazy smile.

"Show me how much you want to stay here, slut?"

And so she had. It had been unlike anything she had ever experienced before. There were no girlish games of seduction, nor flirty looks. He would have none of it. He ordered her to strip, bent her over the back of a chair, and took her violently. That had been only the beginning, however. To her astonishment he had then strapped her arms and legs in place and used a cane on her bottom until the pain was so bad she thought she would die.

It was her introduction to the darker side of sex. And it had changed her irreparably. It had frightened, infuriated, and humiliated her - even while, occasionally - arousing her almost beyond bearing. For the next two years had been forced to allow the principal to use and abuse her, becoming his plaything, and she had hated him for it.

But then she'd got her own back. She'd found out he was similarly abusing another girl, and had planted a tape recorder in his office, recording one particularly nasty session. The tape had found its way to his wife, and to the student radio, where, the announcer being occupied in a side room with his pants around his ankles while Kathleen distracted him, it had played for the entire college.

She had continued to use men to get her way, but that use had become harsher since then, and more ruthless

She took one of the cucumbers out and went to the cellar, then walked downstairs to see Collin Butler hanging weakly from the ceiling. He looked up with a groan, and then dropped his eyes again, gasping.

"Hello, my dear," she said, examining his clipped tongue. Are you enjoying your stay with us? Have you started to understand that you won't be getting your hands on me any time soon? Do you think you're ready to co-operate a little and tell us what we want to know? Or should I perhaps leave you like this all night?"

She reached forward and plucked the clip off his tongue. He let out a cry of pain, quickly drawing it back into his mouth and wincing as he massaged it against the roof of his mouth.

"Poor big man," she said with vastly insincere sympathy. "All those muscles but no way to use them."

"L-let me go and I'll show you what they can do," he croaked.

"But then I'd be a weak little girl and you'd hurt me," she said. "And I just know big men like you would never want to do that."

She fondled his buttocks before walking around the room. She set down the cucumber and lifted a cardboard box off of what appeared to be another, covered in an old rug, then she slid the rug off to reveal a small cage. The cage had heavy bars, and looked too small to contain anything more than a medium sized dog. It was no more than two feet in height.

She dragged it out into the centre of the room and placed it beneath where he hung, then opened up the top.

"Your home for the night, big man," she said.

She went to a nearby table and removed several long straps

before returning to him. She placed two of the straps around his thighs just below his buttocks, cinching them tight, then unclipped his left ankle, holding it in place, and quickly pushing it back against his thigh and strapping it there. She repeated her actions with his other ankle, then released her hold so that he swung down and forward, hanging fully by his wrists.

She went to the wall and turned the crank, and the chain began to lower Collin into the narrow cage. His knees touched the floor first, for the cage had no bottom, only bars. Kathleen adjusted his position as the chain continued to lower him, and his struggle earned nothing but a hard and painful squeeze to his groin.

The front of the cage consisted of the same thick bars as the rest, with the addition of a round hole just big enough to encircle someone's throat. Kathleen removed the strap from his head, and then held his head by the hair as she reached down to swing out the top half of the frame around the hole. Kathleen shoved his head down then swung the top half back so that his head projected through the hole and was locked in place, unable to withdraw into the cage.

She shoved down hard on his back, and then zapped him with the stun gun so that he slumped helpless. His wrists restraints were removed from the spreader bar and pulled back behind him. Kathleen slid a strong metal bar through the side of the cage and out the other, fastening it in place, then pulled each of his arms over the top and back underneath, clipping them to a taut chain, which was clipped to the bottom bars beneath his chest. She removed the dildo from his rectum, eased his backside into position, then thrust a steel bar of almost equal size and thickness into him. This was bolted to the rear of the cage, and would prevent him from wriggling very much.

He lay half on his knees, and she spread them apart, reaching in for his cock and drawing it down. She found a metal plate on the floor. It had a narrow hole in its centre, and a fine line divided the plate in half. She opened the plate, placed it against his groin just above his testicles, then carefully closed it and snapped it in place. She slammed the top of the cage closed and locked it, then attached it to one of the hooks and went to the wall to turn the crank, raising the cage two feet off the floor before locking it in place.

She returned to the cage, reaching up from underneath and pulling the plate which was locked around his cock down, then sliding the bolts in place to hold it firmly locked to the bottom of the cage, his cock projecting downwards. She would do nothing with it at the moment, but had ideas for the future.

He was starting to stir now, and she returned to the wall, raising the cage up a few more feet. His eyes were fluttering now as she returned and she reached up to pet his head as she smiled at him. "You'll have a nice, restful night," she said. "Perhaps in the morning you'll feel more like conversation. Remember, if you make any noise, I'll have to gag you, and that will definitely make for a very sore jaw come the morning."

"Bitch," he groaned.

"Definitely," she said, smiling. "I most definitely am exactly that."

She went to the corner and picked up the cucumber, then returned to him, standing just before him, smiling. She showed him the cucumber, then tilted her head back, slowly pushing the long, thick vegetable through her lips. Inch after inch pushed past her lips, over her tongue, and then began to slide down her throat. She knew that, close as he was, he would be able to clearly see the bulge in the front of her neck as the cucumber pushed downwards. She pushed it down until she held only the base in two fingers, then slowly drew it back up again, and showed it to him.

"See what you have to look forward to if you're nice?" she said teasingly.

She smiled, then set the cucumber just inside the cage, and walked up the stairs, turning off the lights, leaving him swinging there, crushed into the tiny cage, the bars pressing against his legs, shoulders and backside. He groaned as he tried to shift himself into a more comfortable position. There was no comfortable position, and he found that something very hard and very firmly held in place impaled him from the rear. His cock was also trapped somehow below him, and while the weights and clips had been removed, he felt little sense of relief. His flesh still burned from where they had sunk their hard little metal jaws.

"Bitches," he groaned, pure hatred showing in his expression.

He felt a little nauseous as the cage swung, and he tried to keep absolutely still. After a time the swinging almost stopped. But he was inescapably trapped. His wrists were very firmly chained in place, and the bars of the cage were strong enough to hold a lion, never mind him. His knees were jammed up against his chest, and his head was pinned in the hole as though he were a prisoner about to be beheaded.

The bottom of the frame around his neck was flat, but only an inch wide. He found that he could not rest his neck on it for long without it becoming difficult to breath, and so had to hold his head up, or else turn it awkwardly to one side to rest it for any length of time. He did not, of course, sleep at all. Cramps and aches throughout the night tormented his body, so abused during the day, and his frustration and fury at his helpless position almost had him on the edge of tears at times.

He would escape somehow, and they would pay for this. Somehow.

CHAPTER THIRTEEN

Collin felt exhausted and sore all over. He had had nothing to drink since - he could no longer remember. He hadn't eaten since the previous noon. And of course, he had been awake now for almost thirty-six hours. Yet he was to be given no opportunity to relax.

After releasing him from the cage Kathleen promptly hung him from his wrists for an hour or so to put him in the proper frame of mind. She had then proceeded to whip him, first with flogs, which grew increasingly heavy, then with a riding crop. After a half-hour of this he was criss-crossed with welts from thigh to neck. Only on his back, however.

She lowered him enough for his feet to reach the floor, but only the balls of his feet, then left him there for the remainder of the day while she went to work. She had decided that time was on her side, and that time was needed to wear him down sufficiently to be co-operative.

"And how are we this evening?" Kathleen mocked when she returned.

"Fuck you," came the hate-filled response.

She sighed, then fetched the penis gag and forced it into his mouth.

"If you can't say something nice, you won't say anything at all."

She slapped his face then, sending his head flying back, and in response he kicked her, throwing her back across a low stool. He felt a great surge of satisfaction as she picked herself up off the floor, feeling a great delight at putting her on her backside, and hardly noticing the anger in her eyes. He tried to kick her again as she approached, but she moved to his side, forcing his ankles up and back, snapping the ankle restraints to small chains which she fed around his hips and then attached to a tight ring she locked to the base of his cock. She gagged him then, and gazed into his smirking face with cold, hard eyes.

"You're going to learn what happens to those who try to cause me harm," she said icily. "Since it was your feet you used, we'll start with them."

She picked up a heavy riding crop and moved behind him. Collin turned his head nervously, for his back and buttocks were still throbbing and sore from the whipping she had given him that morning. When she brought the crop down, however, it was straight down - against the sole of his right foot. He was startled, and then screamed into the gag as a blast of pain ripped through his foot and leg and dug claws right into his mind.

He thrashed and shook, his foot twisting and jerking. That only served to pull on his already aching cock, however, and he yelled again. Then the crop came down on his other foot, and he screamed anew.

"The foot is quite a tender part of the human anatomy," she said coolly. "Few people seem to realise just how tender."

The crop came down again, with four fast, stinging blows against the sole of his right foot. Collin howled in pain, twisting and writhing and cursing. The pain was horrendous, and it was made worse by the desperate need to keep from trying to yank his foot away. Every time he did the ring bit into his cock, and caused even more pain.

"Even strong men have very tender feet, unless, of course, they're used to spending an awful lot of time on them. Soldiers have stronger feet," she said calmly. "But even their feet are quite tender to something small and thin."

Four fast, sharp blows struck the sole of his left foot, and again he howled starting to feel panicky now as his entire lower legs throbbed with the agony of his feet.

"The interesting thing about the human foot, is that it can

bear tremendous pressure, yet be so soft and pliable in certain spots," she said.

She jabbed the tip of the crop into his sole and he hissed.

Four more fast blows followed then four more on the other foot.

He was sweating desperately by then, almost on the verge of sobbing with frustration, pain and misery.

"Does that hurt?" she asked with a smile. "Darling boy, we've only just begun."

She put down the crop and picked up a cane, then appeared to examine his feet carefully before whipping it down. Collin heard the whistling sound as it cut through the air, and tried to prepare himself for more pain from the soles of his feet. Instead the cane struck his toes - hard. He screamed involuntarily, head thrashing, teeth biting into the gag as his toes caught fire. Another blow followed, and another, and another. Then she switched to his other foot.

She walked around before him, gripping his hair and yanking his head back. She placed her face in close to his and glared at him. "Do you still think you're so tough?" she demanded. "Do you think you can do what you want without regard to what a mere woman desires?"

She released his head and moved behind him. This time she started on the heels of his feet, giving them six blows apiece. Then she moved to the soles, and finally the balls of his feet. The final blows came down on his toes, which were already swelling with pain.

Tears of pain were spilling from his eyes when she moved back in front of them. She wiped one off with a finger and put it in her mouth.

"The taste of pain," she whispered. "Congratulations, you're about one tenth of the way through your punishment. Only nine tenths remaining."

He moaned and rolled his eyes, and she smiled cruelly.

"Would you like to beg me to stop?" she asked. "If you can grovel nicely, and apologise with enough emotion, I may suspend the remainder of your punishment. Would you like to try to do that?"

He nodded his head desperately and she cocked her head to one side, holding a hand to her ear. "What was that? I can't hear you? Speak up?"

His voice was muffled by the gag, but the sound of it was quite audible.

She shrugged and sighed. "Oh well, I gave you a chance."

He cried out, but she moved behind him once again and the blows began to rain down on his feet.

He thought he would go insane. The pain was beyond anything he'd ever felt, and he howled at the top of his lungs, screaming into the gag in nearly mindless agony as she continued to slash the cane down. Hard down onto the helpless, burning soles, heels, and then toes of his feet.

And then she postponed what she called the remaining eighty percent of his punishment to allow him to "rest".

That rest wasn't to be in a position of comfort, however.

There was a six-inch wide, square wooden post in the centre of the room, and he was chained with his wrists up high against it. His ankles had been pulled up and back, each chained at the level of his hips to the opposite sides of the beam. Both wrists and ankles served to support some of his weight, but after hours in that position, most of his weight was now on his tailbone.

There was a metal bar protruding from the beam which pushed out horizontally approximately one inch, then bent ninety degrees and rose a further nine inches - vertically. None of it was visible to the casual observer, for the nine vertical inches were up inside Collin's rectum. Collin's every movement, however slight, was agony as his tailbone ground against the remaining inch.

He was so tired, so exhausted. He was in a semi-daze, the pain and discomfort keeping him from sleeping.

Then she was there before him, the blonde, and he hadn't the energy to spit, to curse her. She smiled at him, and he saw that she was nude. A part of him could not help admire the beauty of her body, and note the stiffness of her brown nipples. A part of him thrummed expectantly at this sight, even as he let his chin fall back to his chest.

Her hands were soft as they moved across his chest, fingers combing through the hair.

"We could have so much fun," she said. "If you'd only be more reasonable."

Her fingers closed around his cock, squeezing and massaging it, and he felt a small surge of anger at himself and his body as it responded, hardening.

"Lovely," she said, looking at it.

He felt a pride in that, but it was a forlorn pride. His feet ached terribly, so much so that even now the ache to his tailbone was only slightly worse. Yet perhaps because of that pain his body and mind were powerfully attracted to any hint of pleasure, to anything which would ease the agony pulsing through his veins. He remembered the sight of her with the cucumber, and his cock twitched in her hand.

"I bet you've pleased many young ladies with this big, stiff cock," she said.

She bent slightly and drew his cock up between her breasts. It twitched against at the warmth and comfort, at the softness of her flesh.

"Would you like me to please you, Collin?" she asked with a flirty little smile. "I bet you would. I bet you'd love to feel my mouth around this big cock of yours."

She straightened, fingers combing through his hair.

"What do you have to fight for, hmm? A pair of wimpy computer types, rich men who think you're nothing but a cheap servant? Or perhaps that fabulous life of wealth you live in your scruffy little flat and dirty little office?"

She squeezed his cock and he barely restrained a groan of pleasure as it throbbed powerfully.

"Come over to the other side, Collin," she cooed. "It's much more fun here."

"Fu-fuck you," he croaked defiantly.

She sighed and shook her head, then let go and drew back. He felt a sense of loss, and a part of him cursed himself for his stupidity even as another part felt proud at telling the bitch off.

He heard a loud cracking noise, and raised his head to see her coming back, holding a roll of ducting tape. She had just drawn two feet of the tape out and was smiling at him in a way which began to shrivel his privates.

"Going to finish the job Yvette started," she said.

And with that she pressed the two-foot strip of tape horizontally across his chest. He looked down dumbly. His chest was quite hairy for he was a strong, powerfully built man and…

She ripped the tape off, and he screamed in shocked pain, jerking violently against the beam.

"Much faster this way," she said.

He was breathless with the pain as she drew the tape out another two feet and slapped it against his chest once more. She smiled, rubbing her hand along the tape to push it in tightly, then ripped it out once again.

Again he howled and jerked, the pain dagger sharp, stabbing into his confused brain. His wrists twisted and pulled against the restraints. His body jerked on the metal rod impaling him. More pain assaulted him, and the blonde placed another strip of tape across his chest.

"N-no!" he sobbed pitifully.

"You forgot to say mistress."

She ripped the tape loose.

He screamed again, now cursing violently, desperately, but she only smiled.

She tore loose two foot-long strips, and placed them over his armpits as his arms were locked up above him. She smiled at him, and then ripped them out simultaneously.

Collin felt as though the flesh were being ripped from his body. It wasn't. Only his body hair was, but he could not imagine that being skinned alive would be more painful. Kathleen pressed the tape against his chest and stomach, against his arms and legs, even along his groin, to catch whatever bits of hair Yvette might have left behind, and each time yanked the tape free with a sadistic force that made him scream in helpless pain.

'Much better now,' she said, running her fingers along his hairless body. "Just like a sweet little girl's body."

She gave his flaccid cock a squeeze, then produced the stun gun once more. Collin felt a wail within him but before it could come out the jolt of power hit him and he gurgled dazedly, his mind scattering as his body went limp.

Whistling softly, Kathleen undid his ankles, letting his feet fall to the floor, then reached behind the beam and released the lever which let the metal probe slide in and back. Yvette came down then, and between them they were able to pull him down from the beam and carry him across the room to the low rack where Peter had lain a few days earlier.

"He barely fits on it," Yvette said admiringly.

Kathleen clamped his wrists down as Yvette finished shackling his ankles, and the two of them watched as the man began to groan and shift weakly.

"I really want to feel that cock inside me," Yvette said.

"Not yet. First we teach him what being a bad boy means, then when he decides to co-operate we teach him how nice it is to be a good boy."

She rolled over the electrical generator, and carefully attached electrical contacts to his testicles and cock. Then as he began to come to, she turned on the machine, allowing a low surge of electricity to set his privates tingling.

"Before we continue with your punishment, which is about two tenths finished now, as I recall, perhaps you would like another opportunity to please us," she said to him. "Tell us all about what Jeffrey Fitzwilliams and Jentech know about us."

Collin was through fighting. He was too exhausted and pain wracked to continue.

"Nothing," he moaned, shaking his head.

"Nothing?"

"Fitzwilliams knows nothing. I haven't got back to him."

"And Jentech?"

"They know it was SpecterWare. They know Peter came from there, and that it must have been him that sabotaged their system."

"Do they know about Yvette and me?"

He shook his head dully.

"Do they know we've stolen information?" she demanded.

"They suspect you might have."

"But no evidence?"

He shook his head miserably.

"How delicious. And nobody knows you're here either."

He shook his head again.

Kathleen looked at Yvette and smiled.

She turned the dial and more power surged through the wires.

He cried out, his body beginning to shake.

"For being so forthcoming, I will eliminate the rest of the punishment you were to receive for kicking me," she said.

"Thank you, thank you!" he panted. "Thank you Mistress."

She turned the power down low, so that once again he felt

only a low buzzing in his privates, a buzzing which set his cock to vibrating.

"There can be other rewards for being a good boy, for cooperating with us. I'm sure Yvette can think of many."

Yvette smiled, reaching for his cock, stroking and massaging it.

"You will, of course, call me Mistress Kathleen, and her Mistress Yvette at all times. Is that clear?"

He nodded his head weakly.

Yvette removed her hand quickly and Kathleen turned the dial up so that he cried out in pain.

"You must always say Yes, Mistress Kathleen, or No, Mistress Yvette. Do you understand?"

Collin felt a small surge of anger, but it fell apart when it hit the fear of pain enveloping him. "Yes, Mistress Kathleen," he whispered.

"Good boy," she said in a patronising tone.

Yvette resumed her expert massage, then, when he was hard, bent and took him into her mouth. She had to spread her jaw painfully wide to engulf his thickness, but was eager to do so. Collin began to groan and sigh in pleasure as she slowly drew more of him into her mouth. It was a rare woman who could get very much of his thick log into them, but Yvette was just that, and soon her lips were wrapped tightly around the base of his cock, the entirety of the shaft and head inside her mouth and throat.

He stared down the length of his hairless body at her and moaned dazedly, watching as her lips slowly rose, as his cock came free. Then she gave him a wicked look, nipped lightly at the throbbing head, and slid forward, taking him into her mouth in one long, smooth movement that had him temporarily fearing she was a strange animal devouring his cock.

He tried to buck up towards her, but the shackles held him too tightly in place. The pleasure and excitement mounted, and he forgot to be either angry or humiliated as the black woman's mouth rode leisurely up and down his thick cock, drawing him closer to the peak of climax. Then it hit, and he cried out, his body stiffening, jerking against the bonds holding him.

Yvette smiled as she rose, patted his cheek, then walked to the stairs. Kathleen patted his head, as well, then turned the crank so that the shackles pulling on his wrists grew more taut. She joined Yvette as they went upstairs, and the light went off.

Slowly, he relaxed. The throb of pain was ever present, and with it hunger and thirst. He did not sleep, but stared sightlessly into the black of the cellar, muddled and barely capable of thought.

Morning came, and with it the two women. The blonde produced a leather hood, and as he lay helpless, pulled it tightly over his head. It strapped and buckled beneath his chin and around his throat, and he could feel the locks click into place. There were no eyeholes, and he could not see as they unfastened him from the table. His arms and legs were useless. They ached terribly from being stretched out for hours. He could hardly think, much less resist, as they dragged him - somewhere, and set him down.

Then his ankles were lifted up, higher and higher. His buttocks slid slowly along the floor, and then they rose as well. His back and then shoulders slid along the floor, until they were raised into the air as well. Then he was hanging upside down once more, the blood beginning to rush to his already confused brain.

A hand caught at his head and pulled his face forward. He felt flesh against his mouth, scented the familiar smell of a woman.

"Lick, boy. Lick well. And perhaps we'll let you have some water."

Water. The thought of it made him moan. He licked frantically, and felt water trickling down against his tongue, trickling over the sex of the woman he was licking. He probed deeply, slurping and sucking at the water, able only to moisten his tongue and mouth, but frantic for more. He licked until his tongue and jaw ached, licked pussies and fingers, and toes. But got little water out of it, certainly not enough to still the craving of his body.

Then he was left alone with his pain and discomfort.

He did not know what day it was. He wished the pain would end.

Instead, it rose. No one spoke. There was no sound, no warning. He did not know how long he had been hanging by then. But suddenly something struck him between the legs, and he cried out in pain. After a third or fourth blow he recognised the sensation as one of the flogs, for she had used it on his back the other day. Now it was striking him between the legs, and the pain burned as the strips snapped and bit at his groin.

After a while it stopped, and he remained blind, unconscious, moaning softly with the new source of pain to his body. More time passed. He had no way of measuring it. His legs were shifted together somehow, and then he was spun and spun and spun so that, were his stomach not entirely empty, he would have vomited. As it was he retched and sobbed and moaned until, after an endless period of time, his body grew still.

More time passed.

The flog bit into his chest, his belly, his abdomen. Then into his back and buttocks at the same time. He howled in pain and thrashed, dancing like a fish on a line. Then it was over and he continued to hang, blinded, groaning and dazed, confused and wracked by pain.

He began to hear soft voices. They promised him pleasure if he obeyed. They told him of the pain which awaited him if he did not. They spoke of the pride of serving strong, beautiful women, and the need to please them. They spoke of the misery of disappointing those women, of the uselessness of resistance, and the freedom of submission.

He did not believe the voices, but then, he did not altogether understand them either. He remained dazed and semiconscious. He could not sleep, for without warning, every few minutes, or sometimes only once or twice an hour, a sharp shock would run into his body from the wire attached to his genitals, keeping him both awake and in a constant state of anxious anticipation.

Time had little meaning. His throat grew dry again, his lips cracked. His flesh was dry and his breathing ragged. He was in desperate need of water, but there was no one to beg it of. No one spoke to him. No one made his or her presence known. He called out but no one answered.

And then someone was there, lowering him to the floor, and he begged them for water, but again they did not answer. After a time he was pulled to his knees. He still could see nothing, and his wrists were locked together behind his back, as they had been for - he did not know how long.

"Slave," a voice said.

A hand was pressed against his head. "You. You are a slave. Do you understand?"

He didn't, was too dazed to understand. His mind blurred and confused.

"You are a slave now. Do you understand?"

Still he did not react, and he felt pain as the fingers returned to his head and yanked it back.

"A slave is one who obeys his master or mistress without question. Are you ready to obey?" the voice demanded.

The word triggered something in him. The word "obey" was associated with pleasure. If he obeyed he would be happy.

He did not know why that was. But it seemed like it was something he had been told or taught.

"Y-yes," he croaked.

"Good. Will you obey your mistress?"

"Yes," he croaked again.

"Say it. Say that you will obey your mistress."

He could barely speak, but managed to get the words out.

"And that makes you a slave. Say that too."

"I am a slave," he croaked.

"Good slave," the voice purred.

He recognised the voice. It was the blonde. He hated the blonde, but that did not seem to matter.

"Would you like a little water, slave?"

"Yes, please, mistress," he begged.

He was raised to his feet and walked some distance, then he felt his wrists released, but only momentarily. He had some thought to pull himself free, but his mind was working very slowly, and by the time he realised what he should do his left arm was already locked up and out above him. His right was in her strong hands, about to be locked in place as well.

For a moment he stood there unmoving, blinking his eyes behind the hood. Then water assaulted him. The water was from a shower, and it was strong indeed. Sharp, needle-like drops rained against his aching chest, belly and groin, and he moaned, trying to twist to one side away from it. The water turned icy cold, and he cried out, shuddering.

Yet his mouth was wide open as he tried to gulp as much of it as possible. It rained down his body until he was trembling with cold, and then abruptly turned scalding - or what felt like scalding - hot. He screamed, closing his mouth, twisting more violently, cursing and calling out, begging them to stop. Yet the hot water continued to shower against him. He groaned helplessly, feeling as though he was melting under the heat. His breathing came in short gasps, and he felt the energy draining from his body.

And then, between one heartbeat and the next, the water turned icy, and he jerked violently, chilled to the bone. Yet his mouth opened again, wide as he could, straining to allow water in. His mouth was starting to lose its desert dryness, but his throat had only felt trickles of liquid.

The water turned hot again and then cold, and then hot once more.

No one spoke to him. No one touched him. The water adjusted back and forth as though a force of nature, at no set intervals, giving him no time to adjust or prepare. It stopped suddenly, and he groaned exhaustedly, head hanging, dripping wet.

"Poor baby," a voice cooed.

He almost fell as his arms were released, then they were locked behind him once again and he was shoved to the floor.

"Feel better, baby?" the voice asked.

The worst of his desperate thirst had been quenched, but only the worst. He had not been able to drink very much water there under the shower. The fine needle spray had made his skin raw but had bounced out of his mouth almost as quickly as it had entered, and he had gulped only mouthfuls.

Something sharp cracked down against his buttocks, and he winced and gasped.

"Move. Crawl."

He crawled on his belly along the floor, going where he was directed. His hips were raised upward by strong hands, and something was pushed slowly into his anus. Hands began to massage his cock, and it hardened. He was slowly sodomised there on his knees; his face pressed against cold stone, jaw slack as expert fingers stroked his erection. He came with an explosive cry of pleasure, and a hand patted his head.

But there would be no rest for him, no time to think, no time of relief to ponder his situation, to attempt to come to terms with it, to even understand it.

His arms were pulled up and back behind his head. His elbows bent around a thick round metal bar. Chains were fastened to his wrist restraints and drawn downwards. His ankles were lifted up, attached to the chains, and he dangled there, groaning from the pain for an uncertain time.

Dazed, he was pulled down from there and made to crawl around the room on hands and knees, then hung by his wrists and flogged anew. Finally he was bound, hog-tied, his back straining terribly, threatening to break, and left in what felt like a tight, hot, airless box.

He was hardly aware of being brought out of that. He regained some semblance of awareness to find himself lying on the cold stone, nimble fingers massaging his aching arms, thighs and back. He was no longer hooded, and could see the blonde smiling down at him as she worked her fingers into his muscles.

"I know that feels sore," she said in a soft, friendly voice. "After your arms and legs have been bound in place for hours it always hurts terribly."

He groaned, but more in relief and pleasure than any ache.

She smiled again, as if reading his mind. "Of course, it also feels wonderful to finally be able to move them."

She kissed him lightly on the chin, then on the side of his throat. She was as naked as him, and straddling his body, and he stared up at her beautiful flesh, entranced. She bent forward, placing her soft breasts against his face, and he chewed and sucked hungrily at her nipples.

She drew back, hands sliding along his aching arms.

"You're so strong," she said admiringly.

He was hard, though barely aware of it, and her soft flesh slid back and forth over his erection, sending a flood of sexual longing through his dazed body. She kissed him gently, and then reached down for his cock, sliding her small fingers along it, raising it, and rising above it. She sank down with a groan of delight echoed by his own as he felt her softness around him.

"You're so big," she groaned, stringing out the words to add emphasis to her statement.

She laid her soft body down over his, kissing him again, and his wrists pulled against their bonds as he sought to enfold her in his arms. His hips lurched upwards and she slipped her tongue between his lips, knees clasping him from either side now as she began to ride up and down.

He was confused anew. She had given him so much pain, treated him so terribly. Yet now she was friendly, pleasing him, her pussy delicious around his cock. His mind, such as it was, clung to that friendliness as a storm tossed seaman would cling to raft suddenly come out of the mist. Warily, he said nothing, did nothing which might displease her.

Their tongues slid sensuously together, their lips moving softly yet passionately, and her body massaged his cold flesh, giving it new warmth.

"Are you my slave, Collin?" she asked, raising her head slightly.

"Y-yes, Mistress Kathleen!" he panted urgently.

She smiled, and he felt a wave of relief and pleasure at having given the right answer.

She kissed him again, her tongue sliding around in his mouth, then sat back up. She produced a cup of water, holding it aloft.

"Will you obey your Mistress?" she asked.

"Yes, Mistress Kathleen!" he exclaimed, staring at the water.

"Say it, slave."

"I will obey your orders, Mistress Kathleen!" he panted.

She smiled, then let him sip a mouthful of water.

"You will obey your mistress?"

He repeated his desperate assurances, and she let him drink again.

She held the cup back, then kissed him again. She worked her body slowly over his, rubbing her breasts against his hairless chest, kissing him.

"Do you love your mistress, Collin?" she asked.

"Yes, Mistress Kathleen!"

"I like to hear it."

"I love you Mistress Kathleen!"

She smiled and he felt another wave of delight.

She let him drink several mouthfuls of water, then set the cup down and began to ride up and down, her pussy muscles squeezing in and out as she slowly ground her hips against him. He moaned, exulting in the pleasure.

"I love you Mistress Kathleen!" he cried, greatly daring.

She smiled, and let him drink from the cup again.

"We're going to have a lovely time together, Collin," she said in satisfaction. "You won't try and disobey me will you?" and she frowned suspiciously.

"No, Mistress Kathleen! I promise, Mistress Kathleen! I love you, Mistress Kathleen!"

She smiled and he trembled in relief, accepted another drink of water, and then watched as her lovely body began to ride up and down on him once more.

CHAPTER FOURTEEN

Yvette slipped her bra up and dropped it back over her shoulders, feeling the wall of male arousal drifting up from the audience with narcissistic pleasure. She crossed the stage, gripping the vertical bar and swinging herself around it, then danced her way back along the edge. Dancing wildly to the African drums, the African Amazon, as they billed her.

Most of the dancers were big titted and small waisted, completely without muscles. She was quite different, and the men were fascinated.

She rolled her tongue along her lower lip, then slid to the stage, then onto all fours. She crawled cat-like along the edge of the stage, giving the nearest men, those in the row only a foot to her left, an ample view of her small, incredibly firm breasts dangling beneath her. She twisted back and around, rose, and danced again, the music pounding into her head, so loud she could hardly hear the obscene shouts from the crowd.

She bent and slipped her thumbs into the waistband of her G-string, then eased it down her legs. A crackle of sexual electricity tore through her at exposing herself to the crowd as she flipped them off. To be naked in front of all these strangers! She writhed and danced, rolled her hips lewdly, and ran her hands slowly up and down her body, taunting them, sneering at them. They all wanted her. They all wanted to do filthy, lewd things to her body. She was so hot, so seductive and exciting. She was sex, forbidden and bawdy, primal, animal sex.

Her set ended and she picked up her scattered clothes to the cheers of the audience and hurried backstage. She was still hot and aroused, and hardly noticed the next girl passing her on her way down the hall. The rest of the strippers were jaded, cynical, almost bored with their jobs, but Yvette was on a mission, and the stripping was only a minor part of it.

Tech Heaven was located amidst the growing collection of high technology businesses in south London, and catered to the exceedingly well-paid computer engineers who worked long hours and had little time for a social life. It had excellent food, a flashy decor, and girls who were not only beautiful, but also amenable to relieving the pressure of a hard day's work. Some of what the girls did was illegal, but the police had more important things to do.

Yvette put on her little leopard print slip-dress and hurried out front into the club. It was time to mingle with the men and chat them up, as the other girls did. Of course, the point of this was supposed to be to sell expensive lap dances. But Yvette had another purpose. She was to bring computer terms into the discussion. There was nothing computer nerds liked better, Kathleen had told her, than to find a beautiful girl who had an interest in computers.

She was specifically to find someone who would respond to her complaints about how difficult it was to order things over the Internet. Kathleen knew men. She knew computer engineers even better. She was betting that any man working on a project which would speed up order entry would rush to tell a pretty girl, especially one like Yvette, who appeared to know nothing about computers what he was up to. And after all, what harm could there be in telling an ignorant stripper the bare outlines of their project?

This was her third week dancing, and she was still slightly embarrassed, yet filled with self-confidence as she moved through the bar. She deliberately sought out the nerdish looking men, the ones with pale faces which showed little time out of doors. She sold a number of lap dances, which both aroused her and helped her finances.

She listened carefully to the conversations around her as she moved, and each time one of the men paid for a lap dance she whispered seductively to him, complimenting him, asking him what he did as she slid her naked body across his. None seemed suspicious, and most were eager to tell what they did, and to pump up the importance of it. She would always introduce the topic by asking if they liked her nipple rings, which she had bought on the Internet.

They had hurt at first, and still throbbed a little. But they did look quite hot and sexy, the two round gold rings dangling from her erect black nipples. And the men seemed fascinated by them.

"Do you like them?" she whispered in a throaty voice, "I bought them on the Internet."

The man was staring wide-eyed at her nipples as she straddled him there in the bar. She was naked now; her dress discarded, and letting her body slide sinuously up and down his as the music pounded behind her. His hands quivered beside him, wanting to rise up and touch her, yet he restrained himself, not daring.

"B-beautiful," he said, his voice squeaking slightly.

She ground herself against him, feeling his erection through his pants, her tongue waggling tauntingly at him as she moved up and down. She let her long hair caress his face as she rolled her head from side to side, then slid upwards, letting her nipples brush gently across his forehead.

She was standing, straddling the chair, her shaved sex just before him.

"I need another ring," she whispered, her hands stroking her sex.

"Y-yes," he gulped.

She finished her dance, and sat on his lap, smiling.

"I really do need another ring," she said in a normal voice, picking up the money from the table where he'd left it. "But I don't think I'll order on the Internet. It's too slow and complicated."

He stared at her, half dazed.

"Well, it'll get better very soon," he said.

"Really?" she cocked her head prettily to one side

"You see, it's bandwidth that slows things down, and the need for a secure connection, which makes it even slower. I work for World In Motion, see, and what we're doing is developing a simultaneous calculation ability which will allow for multi-tasking on access servers. This will..."

She smiled at him as he babbled, trying to understand what he was saying and put it together with some of Peter's babbles, and what Kathleen had told her. This one seemed like a likely target indeed. She leaned forward, silencing him with a light kiss.

"Would you like another dance?" she whispered.

"Y-y-y-es," he gulped.

She brushed her lips across his cheek. "A private dance?"

Lap dances were more expensive in the little booths at the rear of the bar, but more could be done there, more than could be done legally, in fact.

He nodded dumbly, and she smiled, pulling on her dress, then taking his hand and leading him back.

The booths were the size of a toilet cubicle, with a single narrow chair, and a tiny table beside it. Like toilet cubicles the bottom foot or so was open to the sight of those passing by to ensure nothing too naughty was done. Of course, if things were done properly it was difficult to tell what was going on.

And so she straddled the man again, writhing against him in time to the music. Now she pressed her breasts more firmly against his face, her fingers sliding more delicately through his hair. His mouth opened tentatively, as if afraid she would complain, and she smiled encouragingly, pushing her breast forward. He moaned and suckled on it, his tongue lapping at the ring, rasping against her nipple. His hands rose slowly, cupping her firm bottom, then squeezing and kneading it with desperate excitement.

She continued to wriggle slowly, letting him paw and grope her. Her hands undid his trousers and he groaned and gasped, shaking and trembling. She drew out his erection, caressing it with her hands, stroking it against her bare belly. She felt a surge of guilt now, but it was overpowered by her excitement, and by the sense of power she now felt over the man. He was putty in her hands, and she teased him mercilessly.

Money piled up, as, each time she pronounced the dance over, he dropped another ten-pound note on the table. She stood up, legs straight, spread, and bent at the hips, sliding her lips down his chest. She took his erection into her mouth and began to suck. It took little time, mere seconds, and then he was spent and groaning, lying back limp against the chair back.

She straddled him again, cooing and cuddling. "Did you like that, Marty?" she asked.

Marty did, and Marty was relieved at her suggestion they both stay there for a few minutes to recuperate, and Marty allowed himself to be lured back to talking about his project and what it entailed. And as her fingers idly stroked his cock he became erect again, and she talked him into another "dance".

More money went on the table, and she rolled and ground her hips against him, letting his fingers probe at her sex, then pulling his face in so he could lick wildly and inexpertly at her. She moaned softly, only partially faking the excitement she felt. Another ten went on the table, then another, and she was sliding her sex down over his erection, riding up and down as he sucked frantically at her nipple, on the edge of climax herself when he finally came inside her.

Still she wasn't done. Again she persuaded him to rest, to talk, and again her naked body roused him to excitement. Another ten went onto the table, and another, and still another, and now she was riding him again, this time taking him into her anus, shocking him with her own lewdness, with the tightness inside her.

They both came, and she collapsed against him now, as limp as he, groaning exhaustedly as he caressed her body.

And it was he who felt guilty and a little shamefaced as he finally hurried out, out of the booth, and out of the club itself. And well he should, she thought, sitting smugly on his chair and counting the pound notes. Ten pounds a dance, three minutes to the dance. She folded her hands around four hundred pounds, shaking her head in amazement. After years of working for rotten wages for rotten bosses she blessed the day she'd first met Kathleen Hunter.

***

Things were going well for Kathleen. Her engineers were doing a good job of duplicating and fleshing out the information she had been able to purloin from other companies, and even combining the information to come up with new ideas of their own. SpecterWare's stock was at five pounds now, an almost fivefold increase from when she had bought it only two months earlier. Her original fifty thousand investment and the half million pounds of stock she had purchased with it were now worth nearly two and a half million. That was a tidy sum, but it only served to whet her appetite.

First, she paid back the fifty thousand pounds. It was the only money which might have got her into trouble, should an unexpected audit discover it on the books. She still owned just under two and a half million pounds of stock, but owed the broker for the entire cost of the original purchase of a half million. If she cashed in, she'd get two and a half million pounds, less the half million, but never considered it. Instead she decided to increase her holdings. On the basis of the two million pounds worth of stock she owned free and clear the broker allowed her to purchase another twenty million pounds worth of stock.

It hadn't been her original intent to throw herself back into a high-risk position after already realising her ambition of wealth. But now greed overcame her, and she was willing to risk all of that wealth, what she would have once considered an astoundingly large amount of money for yet more.

She was down to owning just ten percent of her stock again, but the profit potential was enormous. If the stock doubled, which she thought it would, it would be worth forty million pounds. She could sell out then, pay off the eighteen million she'd borrowed, and be not merely comfortable, but deliciously wealthy.

She imagined herself with a large estate in the country, servants, a Rolls, and sighed happily. She thought of some other tech stocks which had gone up fifty or more times their original value over three or four years. She allowed herself to consider the possibility of patience, of letting her stock sit for four entire years, but shook her head. SpecterWare was a shadow. Eventually someone would find out that the upcoming line of products was all based on theft. It would only take one accusation from one company to draw attention. Then other companies would come forward, the lawsuits would fly, and SpecterWare's stock would plummet.

Pity the poor fools who had seen the stock rising and climbed aboard, she thought with a smile. They'd all lose their shirts. Already she'd found Internet stock groups buzzing with talk about SpecterWare, the little people beaming about how their paltry investment had doubled or tripled. She imagined the howls of anguish when the stock dropped into the basement and repressed a smile. She felt almost God-like reading them, seeing them giving advice to others on buying more. Little did they know, she thought in amusement. They were on a train headed at a hundred miles an hour straight into the unyielding rock wall of a cliff.

The market was extremely touchy and jittery. Some of the biggest, most respected tech companies in the world had seen their stocks drop twenty and thirty percent in a day just on brief slowdowns in earnings, resignations of CEOs, lawsuits, or government investigations.

Wait until the market found out about SpecterWare.

She was almost awed at the thought, and wondered if she'd bitten off more than she should have. This was going to create rather more of a bang than she'd anticipated. But, she thought with a shrug, she wouldn't be around to listen to the complaints. Her money would be safely in secret accounts in Bermuda and Austria, and she would be sitting on a beach in the Virgin Islands sipping a tangy fruit cocktail and watching the sun set over the Pacific.

She didn't feel much sorrow at the thought of investors losing their shirts either. Most of them were men anyway, and if they had money to play on the stock market they had a lot more than she and her family ever had when she was growing up. Middle class types, no doubt, she thought, lip curling. People who polished their pretty cars on weekends while she was riding the bus, people who went on holiday trips to Italy and America while she sat at home on someone's porch listening to panting, slobbering boys try to talk her out of her panties.

Let them squeal, she thought. She was going to be rich. At last.

She locked up and went home. As she unlocked the door and let herself in her eyes were drawn to the handsome man kneeling a few feet back, smiling adoringly up at her. Collin was nude, his body well shaved. He wore leather restraints on wrists and ankles and straps about his upper thighs, to which his ankle restraints were chained. His hands were free so that he could work while she was away.

He had a set of tasks to accomplish, including vacuuming, cleaning the floors - by hand of course - dusting the furniture which was low enough for him to reach, cleaning the toilet, making the beds, doing the ironing, and other such household chores. He was quite fast on hands and knees now, and moved around quite naturally.

"And have you been a good boy today, Collin?" she asked, petting his head.

"Yes Mistress Kathleen," he said.

"Let's see, shall we?"

She walked about the flat, Collin crawling along at her heels, investigating the tasks he had been set, examining the ironing, and testing the cleanliness of the floors and table tops.

"Very good Collin."

He smiled happily.

"We'll get you a treat for supper tonight."

"Thank you Mistress Kathleen!"

She reached down and unlocked his ankle restraints from the straps around his thighs then helped him stand.

"Now come and help me undress."

"Yes Mistress Kathleen."

He followed her into her bedroom, then undressed her as she stood still, carefully hanging up or folding those items of clothing which did not need laundering, and tossing the others into the hamper. He bent to help her off with her shoes, kissing her feet as he did so, then followed her into the toilet and shower.

He turned on the water, tested it, and then stepped aside to let her in. When she indicated him to, he stepped inside, picking up the soap, lathering up his hands, then soaping up her body. She rinsed, and drew him to his knees, and he eagerly pushed his face in against her groin. He was far more talented now than when she had found him, and his tongue much stronger. It slid up deep inside her and she groaned, grinding herself against him until she climaxed.

He towelled her body dry, brushed and blow-dried her hair, then followed her to her room where, after she picked out clothes, he dressed her. Then they went downstairs. Yvette arrived, and Peter soon after. Peter quickly stripped, and he and Collin made dinner, then while Collin cleaned up Peter knelt on all fours, with Kathleen's feet up on his back while she watched television.

It was a good life, Kathleen decided, and found it suddenly odd how much she was betting on becoming rich, how determined she was to have a life of wealth when this one was already so leisurely and comfortable. Then again, how long could this last?

***

Charles put down the phone, his heart pounding. It had been over three months since he'd first placed his advice about SpecterWare. Now it looked like the house of cards he and Kathleen had built was about to come tumbling down. He called her up quickly.

"Mistress," he said, cupping his hand around his mouth and the receiver. "I just had word from a friend at Jentech. They're petitioning the competition commission to investigate how SpecterWare obtained information on their upcoming product line. There's going to be a legal suit filed as well, any time now, possibly today."

Kathleen felt the words strike her like blows, but she had long been ready for them. "All right, Charles. Make sure everything there is destroyed."

"Yes mistress!"

She hung up and called her broker and had all her shares sold, the funds deposited in her bank. She then called her bank and had all her money sent to an account in Belgium. Then she called Belgium and had the money transferred to accounts in Stockholm and Poland.

There'd be no sitting around playing Miss Innocent on

this one, as she'd originally hoped. Selling everything in a rush like this was going to draw a lot of attention when the investigators started in, and she risked having all her profits confiscated if they stayed where they were.

The delicious part was that her broker did not know who she was. He knew her as Veronica Beacher of Knightsbridge, and the computerised statements he sent each month went to a rented mailbox there. He'd never met her, did not know what she looked like, and would be unable to tell the police anything but that the money had been deposited in an account in that name. Her bank knew no more about her than he did, for she'd used false ID to get the account.

And now it would take weeks of legal wrangling just to be able to find her money, and long before that happened she would have gone to Warsaw and Stockholm, withdrawn the money in cash and, leaving no computer trail to follow, deposited it again in Switzerland.

She could have hoped for more time, for the stock had been rising steadily, but even as it was, she and Yvette were going to be quite nicely off.

"Forty million pounds free and clear," she whispered to herself.

And no taxes on it either. Veronica Beacher would get her tax notices at the end of the year, but let the Inland Revenue try and collect.

By circuitous routes Kathleen's money made its electronic way out of Britain and into a variety of numbered accounts on the continent, then were dispersed to more numbered accounts. Meanwhile she and Yvette packed their things and, in company with Peter and Collin, took a flight to Europe.

SpecterWare's stock started the day at fourteen and a half pounds, and after news of the multiple investigations and lawsuits hit the markets, closed at ten. The next day, as word of the true extent of their behaviour became known, and it was discovered the former president had disappeared, it dropped to four, and the day after to two.

Charles Evans-Finch apologised to his employers for being so dreadfully wrong, for being so easily hoodwinked, and resigned his position, then disappeared. Investigators sifted through SpecterWare's records trying to piece together where all the new information had come from. But the engineers were at a loss. All they knew was that Kathleen Hunter had told them it came from a special think tank she had established in Scotland. And of Kathleen Hunter, there was no sign at all.

Peter Cross, who some accused of being her accomplice, had disappeared as well. And so investigators had no real clue as to what happened or who to lay charges against - presuming they could figure out what charges to lay. There were obviously other people involved, as evidenced by several fast sales of stock just prior to the official announcement of an investigation, but the money had all disappeared. The chairman of the London Stock Exchange spoke darkly of a criminal conspiracy, and vowed to get to the bottom of things.

***

"Raise your bottom more. Very nice," Kathleen said.

"Thank you mistress," Peter said.

He was nude; knees apart, in the sand, while Kathleen sat on a padded chair facing the sea, watching the waves wash slowly ashore.

"Do you know the police are looking for you, Peter?"

"Yes mistress," he said.

"Because you've been a very, very bad boy."

"Yes mistress," he said. "I know I have mistress."

"But I shall protect you, Peter. No one will think to look for you here."

"Thank you mistress," he whispered truly grateful.

Her foot slid between his thighs and rubbed against his cock, which was already semi-erect. It grew harder and she chuckled appreciatively.

"You're such a sweet little slave boy," she said.

"You're a wonderful mistress, Mistress," he replied.

"Of course I am," she said.

Yvette came and sat in the chair beside her and Kathleen raised an eyebrow.

"Raining again in London," Yvette said.

"Apparently so," Kathleen replied, nodding at the radio beside her on the sand.

The World Service of the BBC finished its weather report for the London area, then went on to speak of the latest political scandal, the girl Prince William was supposedly dating, then finished up with a brief item on the continuing investigation into the bizarre doings at a small London technology company. So far all the principals had made themselves scarce, and the authorities were at a loss.

"I wonder whatever happened to Jeffrey," Yvette said, looking out at a sailboat sliding gracefully across the waves just below the horizon.

Kathleen shook her head, scowling out to sea. "You heard what the Times said. The poor boy's been driven loony. They caught him masturbating on the board room table to pornographic images of himself being spanked by some mysterious women."

"Shocking."

Yvette snapped her fingers, and Charles rose quickly from where he knelt in the soft sand.

"Yes mistress?" he asked eagerly.

He wore the slimmest of G-strings, and seemed to have a constant erection. Yvette gave it a squeeze, then handed him her glass.

"More wine, little one," she ordered.

"At once mistress!"

He hurried past her into the house.

Kathleen looked past him to where Collin waited, similarly dressed, eager for his own chance to serve.

The waves washed ashore and she looked past them, imagining she could see over the horizon, far to the north and east, to where people shivered cold and wet in bus queues, waiting to go to dreary jobs. Poor people.

Yvette motioned Collin forward and he crawled across the sand. He seemed to prefer crawling now, and only rose when he was told to. She motioned him in front of her chair and he knelt as Peter was so that she could rest her feet on his back.

"We need another slave," Yvette said. "So we can have two apiece. Where do you think we should look?"

"They're all around us, my dear. Weak little men desperate to give us anything we want."

Yvette nodded. That was especially true now that they were wealthy.

But then, men were so cheap.

THE END.

Title: Mistress Blackheart **ISBN:** 1 897809 94-8
Author: Francine Whittaker **Price:** £5.99
Pub. Date: 20th Feb '01 **Pages:** 224

Imprint: Stiletto
Publisher: Silver Moon

STORY:

Always outrageous and highly sexed, Ali returns from an extended trip to Europe with two aims in life. The first is to set up her own "house of correction", having learnt the art of sexual domination at the hands of the woman known as The White Goddess. The second is to completely dominate her old friend, Leigh McFarlane. But things don't quite go to plan and just when Ali gains total control of Leigh, she finds she has to fight off the White Goddess herself.

GENERAL:

Containing punishment, bondage and humiliation of both men and women alike, this book will appeal to female and male readers. With a sadistic main character whose aim turns to obsession, this book's plot twists and turns to reach its conclusion.
The female author adds her deep knowledge of feminine sexual thinking and womanly needs to make this a most readable and exciting book.

Title: Military Discipline **ISBN:** 1 897809 93-X
Author: Anna Grant **Price:** £5.99
Pub. Date: 20th Mar '01 **Pages:** 224

STORY:

A collection of six war/military theme female domination stories cleverly written by a female author most knowledgeable inthis field. Uniforms, discipline, capture, and torture abound in this delightful set of stories varied to suit all tastes. From the Russian frony in WW II to pirates in the Caribbean and onto the modern paint-balling scenarios these stories hold all the essential ingredients expected in fem-dom novels.

GENERAL:

Much research has been carried out on this book to ensure detailed acccuracy from this most knowledgable author. This book will appeal to many be they forces orientated or not but will certainly appeal to the great many uniform lovers in the general reading public.

Title: Tomb of Pain   **ISBN:** 1 897809 92 1
Author: Arabella Lancaster-Symes   **Price:** £5.99
Pub. Date: 20th April '01   **Pages:** 224

STORY:

The wicked Erika Wolf is the hunter and Lady Susanís daughter, the young and naive Hannah, is her prey. Known for her liking for the female flesh in sexual terms Erika uses all of her charm, personality and demanding ways to try to ensnare the young girl. Hannahís mother, Lady Susan, had already fallen into the trap and others too follow the painful and demeaning route to the Tomb of pain. Can Lady Susan save her daughter from the same fate or does her daughterís discovery and practice of sexual deviations of sex forestall her mothers rescue attempts?

Archaeology and ruins in a very different setting indeed as too are the practices contained within. The tomb of pain it is named and suffering abounds in this well written book by one of our most popular authors.

GENERAL:

A novel of female domination over mainly female subjects. This author is one of our most popular, his titles are sought readily by his large following of reading fans. This novel will most certainly not disappoint them.

The cover photograph for this book and many others are
available as limited edition prints.
Write to:-

Viewfinders Photography
PO Box 200,
Reepham
Norfolk
NR10 4SY

for details, or see,

www.viewfinders.org.uk

All titles are available as electronic downloads at:

http://www.electronicbookshops.com

e-mail submissions to:
Editor@electronicbookshops.com

STILETTO TITLES

1-897809-99-9   Maria's Fulfillment *Jay Merson*
1-897809-98-0   The Rich Bitch *Becky Ball*
1-897809-97-2   Slaves of the Sisterhood *Anna Grant*
1-897809-96-4   Stocks and Bonds *John Angus*

Due for release January 20th 2001
1-897809-94-8   Mistress Blackheart Francine Whittaker

Due for release February 20th 2001
1-897809-93-X   Military Discipline Anna Grant

Due for release March 20th 2001
1-897809-92-1   Tomb of Pain Arabella Lancaster-Symes

Due for release April 20th 2001
1-897809-91-3   Slave Training Academy Paul James

Due for release May 20th 2001
1-897809-90-5   Submission to Desire A. Lancaster-Symes

Due for release June 20th 2001
1-897809-89-1   The Governess Serena Di Frisco

Due for release July 20th 2001
1-897809-88-3   Stern Manor Denise la Criox

Due for release August 20th 2001
1-897809-87-5   Six of the Best (Anthology) Various